TERROR RIDES THE WEST WIND

Bill Raymond, private detective, gets one of the toughest assignments of his career when he sets foot in the small, mid-western town of Lynx Falls. Dorothy Peters, lovely daughter of the man who has brought gang law to Lynx Falls, commissions Raymond to clean up the town. He has orders to stir up trouble, to set one gangster against another until they liquidate each other. Together with Dot Peters and Jerry Goodrich, editor of the Lynx Falls 'Gazette', Raymond is caught in the cross-fire

STAFFO

SYDNEY J. BOUNDS

TERROR RIDES
THE WEST WIND

Complete and Unabridged

LINFORD
Leicester

Originally published in paperback in 1951

First Linford Edition
published 2005

British Library CIP Data

Bounds, Sydney J.
  Terror rides the west wind.—Large print ed.—
Linford mystery library
  1. Detective and mystery stories
  2. Large type books
  I. Title
  823.9'14 [F]

  ISBN 1–84395–750–7

Published by
F. A. Thorpe (Publishing)
Anstey, Leicestershire

Set by Words & Graphics Ltd.
Anstey, Leicestershire
Printed and bound in Great Britain by
T. J. International Ltd., Padstow, Cornwall

This book is printed on acid-free paper

1

Bill Raymond drove into Lynx Falls from the east as the sun was going down behind the hills back of the town. Factory smoke-stacks clustered to the south, rearing dingy grey chimneys against a blood-red sky. A haze of dust settled across the town.

Raymond was not impressed by his first view of Lynx Falls. The bulk of the town was tightly jammed in a bowl between mid-western hills, with newer suburbs straggling out to wooded slopes. The streets were too narrow, like ugly slits between dirty brick houses; only on the outskirts was there any freshness, any space for breathing clean air.

Main Street ran north-east to south-west like a crooked spine propping up the town; Central Plaza, at the junction of Main and Columbus Avenue, would have been a pleasant square thirty years ago; now, the trees were sooty and the sidewalks unswept. It was still the hub from which the town of Lynx Falls radiated, but a neglected hub, left there to do a job without anyone bothering about it. City Hall occupied one corner of Central Plaza. That, too, was a faded, smoke-grimed hulk of a building.

Raymond waited for the traffic lights to change, then tooled his Cadillac up Main, heading north. Three blocks from Central, the Palace Hotel put out a front that had once been white stone and gilt; you'd have to scrape off many layers of dirt to find either the white stone or the gilt to-day. The awning over the entrance porch had a tear in it and the man on duty had a button missing from his uniform. The other buttons were tarnished.

Bill Raymond parked the Cadillac and hefted his suitcase through the foyer. It was a long time since the tiled floor had been washed. The air of despondency seemed to have spread to the clerk behind the desk.

The clerk had dull eyes set in a pasty face and he looked at Raymond as if hotel guests were just a nuisance to him.

2

'I want a room and a bath,' Raymond said. 'And a hot meal. I don't know how long I'll be staying — maybe quite a while.'

The clerk didn't seem interested. He pushed the register across without a word. Raymond signed it and the clerk said:

'Room No. 107, first floor front. Dinner in an hour. Okay?'

Raymond nodded, caught up his suitcase and started up the stairs. The Palace hadn't got around to an elevator yet. 107 had faded wallpaper and a broken washstand. The sheets were clean, but threadbare. There was a chair, and a table that rocked because the legs had warped. It wasn't a luxury suite.

Raymond unpacked his bag and located the bathroom. He spent half an hour soaking and came out refreshed, his travel-weariness gone.

He put on a clean shirt, knotted his tie, felt in his pocket for cigarettes. He was right out. Downstairs, the bar was as dead as the rest of Lynx Falls. The bartender had been a fat man but he was wasting away; his flesh hung in limp folds and he mopped the counter without enthusiasm.

Raymond bought a pack of cigarettes and lit up. He drank a slug of whisky and talked to the man behind the bar.

'What part of town is Northwood? I'm looking for a Miss Peters?'

The man's face changed. It became wary.

'You know her? You got business with her?'

His tone indicated he wasn't in favour of strangers who had business with Miss Peters. Raymond ignored his questions, asked again:

'Where can I find her?'

The bartender was reluctant to answer. At last, he said:

'She has a large brownstone house, north end of town. Follow Main out past the old town and you'll find Northwood. What you want with her?'

Raymond parried: 'You don't seem to like Miss Peters. How come?'

The bartender went on mopping the counter without enthusiasm. His eyes never lifted, never met Raymond's, and

4

his voice was low.

'Lynx Falls was a nice little town before her old man arrived and the crooks took over. She owns most of it now. She isn't popular with honest folks.'

Raymond digested that thoughtfully.

'Her old man's dead?'

The barman nodded.

'Six months ago — a stroke. He came out to Lynx Falls when the boom started, worked hard, bought up most of the town. We used to call it Petersville. Then the crooks started in. Old Peters wasn't particular who he hired to do his dirty work; all he wanted was to run things his way. But his gunmen got other ideas; they wanted to run the town *their* way — and Peters found he couldn't get rid of them. He'd bitten off more than he could chew.'

'So Peters was crooked? Why hold that against the girl?'

The barman stopped wiping the counter. He raised his eyes to Raymond's, and said:

'She's his daughter, a chip off the old block. It's in her blood.'

Raymond didn't say any more. He

didn't tell the barman he was a private dick from New York, that Miss Peters had sent for him, that she'd enclosed a retainer of five thousand dollars. He thought there was more to Miss Peters and the Lynx Falls set-up than the barman knew. If the girl was crooked, she wouldn't be hiring a private detective . . . or would she?

That gave Raymond something to think about over dinner. He needed something to take his mind off the nearly cold potatoes, the limp cabbage and stringy hanks of beef. The town's general air of dissipation seemed to have reached the kitchen. Raymond washed the meal down with a Lager and went out to his car.

The sun had set now. Shadows crawled across Main Street; the street lighting was typically inadequate to cope with the encroaching darkness. The side alleys were black, unlighted and uninhabited. The moon had started to rise but its pale beams succeeded only in bringing a gaunt and ghostly air to Lynx Falls.

Bill Raymond drove his Cadillac up Main. There were few people about after dark and those seemed headed for the nearest saloon. A lone cop patrolled his beat; he was hatless and his tunic buttons were dull. Apparently the force, too, had caught the disease.

Beyond the drab apartment blocks, the road widened and a few trees sprouted green leaves to show that Nature was fighting back. The road swung in a long curve, lined with a better class of residential house; further out, the houses were larger and newer, with flowered lawns and goldfish pools. Northwood was the home of the upper income brackets.

He had no difficulty in finding the house he wanted. Wrought-iron gates carried a large sign with the one word:

PETERS

He swung the Cadillac through the gates and along the gravel drive to a rambling brownstone house. The lawns were well-kept, the hedges and shrubbery neatly trimmed. Even if the Peters family did own Lynx Falls, the rot hadn't started from here.

There was a car parked outside the front porch, a green coupé. Raymond stopped beside the coupé and went up the stone steps. On each side of the door, scrubbed stone lions mounted guard. He hung on the bell rope and listened to distant chimes.

The door opened silently and a butler asked:

'Yes sir? Can I help you?'

Raymond passed across his business card. He said:

'Miss Peters asked me to come out.'

The butler wasn't impressed. He showed Raymond into the hall with quiet dignity. He was strictly the old family retainer.

'Miss Peters is engaged, sir. If you'll wait here, I'll find out when she can see you.'

The butler went away, knocked on an oak panelled door and passed through. Raymond heard voices from inside: the voices of a woman and two men. They seemed to be raised in argument.

The hall was wide and tiled in pale blue and cream. A stairway curved upwards to a balcony. Between stone pillars, a large mirror reflected the passage leading to the back of the house.

The mirror also showed that Bill Raymond was tall and lean with a bronzed face and light brown hair His grey suit was old enough to conform to his muscular frame; it accentuated his athletic litheness, his long legs and broad shoulders. His face had a kind of rugged handsomeness that some women find attractive; an interesting face with brown eyes over a straight nose, a humorous mouth and a square jaw. There was something about him to remind you of a giant cat, the sleek suppleness of a panther.

The mirror showed him lighting a cigarette as the oak door opened and two men came out. One was the butler; Raymond concentrated his attention on the other man. He wasn't as tall as Raymond, and his face was dark to the point of swarthiness. His nose was aquiline above thin lips. Once, he had been strikingly handsome but that was before someone had used a knife on his face.

The scar ran from the sideburn below his right ear, slashing down a dark cheek to his mouth. It gave him a sinister appearance that was not disguised by his white teeth, his superficial smile. He had black, greasy hair and high cheekbones, a man with Latin blood in his veins. He wore a black drape suit with pointed shoes, a soft white shirt and black bow tie.

The man with the scar looked at Raymond. His voice was flat as he said:

'Lynx Falls isn't healthy for strangers. Get out of town while you're still in one piece.'

He went by Raymond with short, mincing steps and opened the front door. He paused, swung round to snap at the girl who had come into the hall:

'You'd better marry me, Miss Peters — I'm a man who gets what he wants, one way or another!'

He closed the door behind him. Bill Raymond looked at his client. He raised his eyebrows, drawled:

'An original method of proposing marriage. I should imagine you can hardly wait to accept.'

Dorothy Peters laughed.

'I hope you took a good look at Nick Traill. If you take the job I'm going to offer you, you'll be seeing a lot more of him.'

Raymond smiled easily.

'That puts me right off,' he said. 'I could wait a long time without going crazy if I didn't set eyes on Scarface.'

He spent a pleasant few minutes studying the girl and decided he'd sooner look at her any day. Dorothy Peters was short and inclined to plumpness. She wore a simple dress of pastel green and filled it in a way that was purely feminine. She had wavy, dark hair and full lips, richly carmined. Her eyes were dark under long lashes and her skin was smooth and pink.

Bill Raymond had seen many beautiful girls but he couldn't remember meeting one who attracted him more. There was a helplessness about her that made him want to protect her. He was filled with a sudden desire to take Miss Peters in his arms and tell her he'd take care of her.

He restrained the feeling; a private detective doesn't make passes at his clients — not if he wants to stay in business.

'If you'll step into the library, Mr. Raymond,' she said, 'we can talk over a drink. And I want you to meet Jerry Goodrich.'

Raymond stepped through the oak panelled door into the library. It was a large room with the walls covered by shelves of books; at one end there was a desk littered with papers; at the other, a log fire with chairs drawn around it.

Jerry Goodrich rose to greet him. He was about twenty-five; four years younger than Raymond, two or three older than the girl. He wore thick-lensed spectacles and had a slight hump behind his shoulder. His hair was curly and his face freckled. He was dressed in brown and smoked a curved pipe.

Dorothy Peters introduced them.

'Jerry is editor of the Lynx Falls *Gazette*. Mr. Raymond is a private investigator from New York — I hope he will help us.'

Raymond mumbled a greeting half-heartedly: he had just discovered that the girl had a freckle on the side of her snub nose. The discovery fascinated him.

Goodrich said: 'Glad to meet you, Raymond. I hope you're going to take this job — we need help badly.'

Miss Peters studied Raymond carefully. She seemed impressed with what she saw. She said:

'I think Raymond is our man. I don't think he'll scare easily.'

Bill Raymond grinned and sat down in front of the fire.

'What scares me most,' he said, 'is that you won't offer me a drink!'

Goodrich fixed three drinks. The girl took gin and lime in a large quantity; Raymond figured that was out of character. She must be on edge about something.

He sipped his whisky and enjoyed it. An expensive brand with a kick to it. He said:

'Suppose you tell me why you think I'm worth a five grand retainer?'

Goodrich drank silently. The girl sat

down opposite Raymond. She had nicely plump legs in gossamer-sheer nylon.

'You're worth a lot more than five grand — if you're tough and honest, and not afraid of being shot in the back. I need someone who knows his way around and can take care of men who murder for fun if they can't find anyone to pay them for it. Which they can in Lynx Falls.'

'Sounds interesting,' Raymond said casually. He discovered that his cigarette had gone out; he relit it and blew a smoke ring with practised ease.

Dorothy Peters went on: 'I own most of Lynx Falls — on paper. But I have as little control over my property as I have over the weather. You see, Mr. Raymond, my father was a ruthless man; he knew what he wanted — money and power. And he set out to make Lynx Falls his own. He wasn't particular about some of the methods he used, unfortunately . . .'

She sipped her gin and lime and stared at the carpet.

'I was too young to know what was going on. My father hired gunmen to run the town for him; honest men didn't have a chance to compete. But a time came when the gunmen got ideas of their own — they turned on my father and told him they were finished with him, that they were going to run things their way.'

She looked Raymond in the face.

'I don't want you to think my father was just a crook. He despised the men who worked for him. He started off to buy up the town . . . and the first touch of power went to his head. Nothing would satisfy him after that. So he resorted to methods outside the law to speed up his conquest of Lynx Falls. He succeeded too.'

Bill Raymond lit a fresh cigarette. He was beginning to feel sorry for the girl; she must have had a shock when she discovered what her father had been doing.

'When dad died, six months ago, I learnt what had been going on. This house, all the money I possessed, had come from crooked deals. It was blood money, forced out of honest people by hired gunmen. Then I found there wasn't anything I could do about it — my hands were tied. Although I have a controlling interest in all the important undertakings in town, that power is purely theoretical. It is the gangsters who really own Lynx Falls.'

'Except the *Gazette*,' Jerry Goodrich interjected.

Miss Peters ignored him.

'I want to set things right with the people of this town,' she said. 'I want to get rid of the crooks, to see that civil power goes back into the hands of honest men. I don't mind losing my share of the loot — I'd sooner not have blood on my hands — but I *do* want to clean up Lynx Falls.'

She turned her dark eyes on Raymond, and said:

'I want you to take on the job of running these crooks out of town. It won't be easy — they'll try to kill you. But it's got to be done. Mr. Raymond, will you take the job?'

Raymond drew on his cigarette. It was the most fantastic proposition he'd ever received. For one lone operative to attempt to clean up a town run by gangsters seemed to him like a simple way to commit suicide. But there was something about the set-up that appealed to him — and about Dorothy Peters too.

The girl said: 'I have quite a lot of money — and I don't mind how much the job costs. You can name your own fee, but it must be a thorough job. I don't want one crook left in Lynx Falls. Not one. And I don't care how you do it. Well, will you take the job? Have I hired you, Mr. Raymond?'

2

There was a moment of silence in the library. Jerry Goodrich puffed on his curved pipe, offering no comment on the girl's strange proposal. Dorothy Peters finished her gin and lime; she set down the empty glass and looked at Raymond with pleading eyes. Bill Raymond smiled at her, waved away cigarette smoke.

'I'll need to know one or two more things before committing myself,' he drawled. 'For instance, you have a police force in this town — why don't they do something? Why don't you go to the Chief of Police and demand action?'

Goodrich laughed harshly.

'You don't know Archer,' he said.

'Archer is Chief of Police,' the girl explained. 'My father put him in office — and he's one of the men behind the crooks in this town. The gangs can get away with anything because Archer is paid to let them. If I went to him, he'd smile politely, agree with everything I said — and laugh when my back was turned. He won't raise a hand against the men who pay him.'

'Who runs the gangs?' Raymond asked.

Miss Peters ticked them off on her fingers, one by one.

'Mick Traill — you've met him. He owns a gambling house at the south end of town. Smitty runs a pawnshop on Columbus Avenue; he acts as fence for the gangs, distributing all the hot stuff. Then there's O'Connor, a bootlegger — he supplies the whole town with hooch; you'll find him on Grant Street. Dr. Fawkes has a house down by the lake where he runs seances; blackmail is just a sideline with him. Underhill is my lawyer; he has my property wrapped up so I can't do what I like with it — he has a finger in a good many pies. Look for him out at Delaware Park, west on Columbus.'

'Don't forget Elsa, *dear* Elsa,' Goodrich remarked.

Dorothy Peters flushed.

'What about Elsa?' Raymond said.

'She's Traill's girl friend.'

Raymond grinned.

'Lynx Falls is sure one swell town!'

The girl said: 'Between them, these people run Lynx Falls. And it's got to stop.'

'You'll have the *Gazette* behind you,' Goodrich said. 'I intend to start a clean-up campaign. There are still enough honest citizens left to support us, but we must have a leader, someone to set the ball rolling. That's where you come in, Raymond.'

Bill Raymond finished his drink. He stubbed out his cigarette. He asked:

'What was Traill doing here? Apart from proposing that you marry him, Miss Peters?'

'That dago!' Goodrich burst out. 'If he tries to force his attentions on Dot, I'll go gunning for him myself. He isn't fit to clean her shoes!'

Dorothy Peters said: 'Traill wanted to marry me because he thought that, between us, we could clean up. He isn't interested in *me*.'

Jerry Goodrich snarled: 'Don't be too sure. The way he was looking at you, I wouldn't trust — '

The girl laughed softly, placing her hand on his.

'Don't be silly, Jerry. I can take care of myself so far as Nick Traill is concerned.'

Raymond watched Goodrich closely. The editor was acting like a man in love. He wondered if the girl felt about Goodrich that way; she wasn't wearing an engagement ring, but the editor's interest was obvious. Raymond felt a pang of jealousy.

She saw the way he was looking, and said:

'Jerry asks me to marry him regularly every month, Mr. Raymond. And I say 'no' just as regularly. He's a good friend — but I'm not in love with him.'

Bill Raymond realized she was speaking directly at him. His pulse beat quicker. He knew instinctively that she was attracted to him. Their eyes meet; the girl lowered hers.

He directed the conversation back to a less personal level.

'How about the state police?'

She shrugged.

'They remember my father. I'm not popular around these parts; they probably thought I just wanted to seize the reins myself. I even tried going to Washington direct. I got the promise of an investigation, but you know how it is. Red tape. It will be months, possibly a year or more, before they get around to doing anything. That's why I decided to hire a private detective, to get things moving.'

Raymond watched the freckle on the side of the girl's snub nose. He found it quite delightful. He said:

'Do you have any plan of campaign?'

She leaned forward, eagerly.

'Both Archer and Traill want to cut each other out. They both want complete control over the town. O'Connor doesn't like Traill because the dago interferes with his business. None of them trust each other. It should be possible to play one gang against another, till the top men are eliminated. The small fry will be easy enough. We can deal with them afterwards.'

Bill Raymond grinned. Dorothy Peters was a girl with ideas; he guessed she took after her father.

'Playing one end against the other, then against the middle, is liable to be dangerous,' he pointed out. 'There may be a little lead thrown around — and we'll be in the crossfire.'

Miss Peter's dark eyes flashed.

'Scared?' she challenged.

'I'm shaking in my shoes!' Raymond retorted.

Jerry Goodrich came in with:

'This is getting us nowhere. Are you going to take the job, Raymond?'

'I'll think about it,' Raymond replied quietly. 'I'll stay in Lynx Falls a couple of days and nose around. If I like the idea of spring-cleaning the town, I'll take it. I'll let you know, Miss Peters.'

He rose to his feet, stretching. The girl admired his panther-like suppleness, his broad shoulders.

'I hope to see you again,' she said.

Jerry Goodrich followed him to the door.

'Can you give me a lift into town?' he asked. 'I've got to look in at the *Gazette* office.

Raymond said: 'Sure.'

They went through the hall to the door. Miss Peters called: 'See you tomorrow, Jerry.'

'Yeah. Goodnight, Dot.'

The door closed behind them. Moonlight bathed the front of the house, sending ripples of silver across the lawn. The green coupé had gone; Traill's car; Raymond made a mental note to watch out for it.

He slid between the wheel of his Cadillac. Goodrich got in beside him and the car moved forward, out of the drive, on to the road back to town. Neither man spoke for a time. Goodrich sat behind his curved pipe, slightly humped, his spectacles gleaming in the moonlight. Raymond was thinking about Dorothy Peters and the crooks who ran Lynx Falls, when the editor spoke:

'I guess you're wondering if Dot's on the level, or if she just wants you to get rid of the gangs so she can play her father's game.' He drew a deep breath. 'Well, I can tell you she's okay. She took it bad when she found out what her old man had been up to. Then she stuck out her chin and said: 'Jerry, I'm going to square things up with the people of Lynx Falls. I owe it to Dad.' She'll back you to the limit if you take this job.'

'Maybe,' Raymond said shortly. 'I'm in the habit of making up my own mind. Let it ride, Goodrich.'

There was another silence. The Cadillac moved out of Northwood, leaving the upper income brackets to their spacious lawns and ornamental gardens. Lynx Falls came at them with bleak apartment houses and grimy smoke-stacks; even the moonlight appeared greyer on the side-walks between sooty trees.

Raymond headed down Main Street. The *Gazette* office was a little beyond the Palace Hotel, on the opposite side. The Cadillac stopped and Goodrich hopped out. He turned, thrust his head back inside and said:

'I'm not dumb, Raymond — I saw how you two were looking at each other. You're the first man Dot's ever fallen for and, if you hurt her, God help you. I love that girl more than life. You'd better be worthy of her, that's all.'

He slammed the door and disappeared into the newspaper office. Bill Raymond grinned; he thought Goodrich would be a useful man to have on his side if trouble broke out. Which it might.

He reversed the Cadillac, crossed the street. There was a light in the window of a shop near the hotel. A florist's shop. Raymond thought it would be nice to send Miss Peters a bouquet, just to let her know his interest wasn't entirely professional. He stopped the car and went into the shop.

The door opened without a sound, that was why the two persons in the shop didn't hear him. The florist, an elderly woman with greying hair and lines of worry about her eyes, said:

'I can't pay any more — I can't. It was only last week you took fifty dollars. Now — '

Raymond looked at the man. He was hatless, wearing a police uniform with dirty buttons. A night-stick swung from his wrist. The cop growled:

'Now see here, you'll pay up or else. We want another ten bucks a week — and don't say you can't afford it. That won't wash. You do plenty of good business with all the funerals there are in town. Maybe the next one'll be yours!'

The old woman looked up and saw Raymond. Her eyes were frightened. The cop spun round. He blustered:

'Who in hell are you? Strangers hadn't better poke their noses in Lynx Falls — it ain't healthy.'

'Maybe your Chief of Police would like to know that one of his men is working the old protection racket?' Raymond suggested.

The cop sneered: 'You think he don't take his cut?'

Raymond said: 'Then maybe I'll handle you myself — I don't like men who threaten old women. I don't like cops who go crooked. And I don't like your ugly mug!'

The cop flushed. He was a burly man with a red face and ham-like fists. He wore cauliflower ears with a flattened nose. He looked as if he could take care of himself — but there was something about Raymond's lean figure, his square jaw and glinting brown eyes that made him step back.

'You made a mistake, mister,' he grunted, and slid round Raymond to the door. He went out hurriedly.

Raymond turned to the florist. He said:

'Are all the cops in this town as crooked as that one?'

She didn't answer. Her eyes were still frightened. Her hands twitched nervously.

Raymond said: 'You don't have to be afraid of me — I'm nothing to do with any Lynx Falls outfit.'

'You'd better get out of town quick,' she said. 'Healey won't forgive you for that. He'll be after you — him and all his mob. Police!' She spat in disgust. 'Gangsters, that's what they are!'

Raymond remembered what he'd come for. He mentally docketed the information about Healey and the police force of Lynx Falls, and said:

'I want you to send some flowers out to Miss Peters first thing in the morning. Enclose this card.'

He handed the florist a pasteboard card with his name printed on it. Just his name; this one didn't say — Private Investigations. He rustled a five dollar bill.

The old woman shook her head.

'Keep your money. You just saved me ten dollars — I'll take it out of that. But I'd stay away from Miss Peters, young man. She isn't a nice girl.'

'Oh,' said Bill Raymond. 'What have *you* got against her?'

'Her father ruined this town,' the old woman said bitterly. 'His blood runs through her veins.'

'Yeah, but that doesn't mean she's bad too. Make it red roses will you? Goodnight.'

He went out to his car, drove to the hotel and parked it. The tiled foyer was still dirty; the clerk with the pasty eyes looked at Raymond as he passed on his way to the stairs. He didn't say anything, but his dull eyes never left Raymond till he was out of sight. Raymond wondered what he'd done to rouse interest in the clerk. He found out when he reached the top of the stairs and opened the door of 107. He had visitors.

There were three men in the room. Two were uniformed cops, with creased tunics and dirty buttons. One sprawled full length on the bed, smoking a cigarette; the other sat on a corner of the table, swinging a night-stick. Both of them looked as if they'd be more at home in convict's clothes.

The third man was short and stout, with a flabby, purple face and tiny beads of eyes almost hidden under rolls of fat. The eyes were bright with animal cunning. A cheroot protruded from his mouth and a brown stain ran down his chin. His hands were small, like a baby's, with short, podgy fingers. He was dressed in a soiled blue serge suit that hung loosely over his corpulent belly.

He said: 'I'm Archer, Chief of Police. You Raymond?'

Bill Raymond stared at the three men, at his clothes scattered on the floor. His suitcase had been forced open in the search.

'Do you usually welcome visitors to Lynx Falls this way?' he asked.

Archer had Raymond's Luger in his fat

hands. He toyed with the gun, watching Raymond with his beady eyes.

'What you doing in Lynx Falls? Why did you run out to see Miss Peters? You got a license for this thing?'

Raymond lit a cigarette, drew on it, flicked the match across the room. He kept his back to the closed door, so no-one else could come in, so the cops couldn't get behind him. He wasn't sure yet how he wanted to play this trick. He flashed his gun license, said:

'I like your town. The air's so pure. And I might ask Miss Peters to marry me. Anything wrong in that?'

The cop on the bed laughed.

'A wise guy. Let's pull him in for resisting arrest.'

The cop with the night-stick said:

'Let me work on him a little.'

Archer handed Raymond back his license. His voice had a squeak in it.

'Mr. Raymond's a private dick. Ain't that lovely?'

Both cops laughed as if it was the funniest thing they'd heard since Mother's Day. They took it in turns to jeer:

'I heard a story about a private dick — turned out he was honest. Can you beat that?'

'I can't believe it. Did you hear about the snoop who got a cold in the eye from looking through keyholes? He had to give up divorce cases.'

'Maybe not all private eyes go in for blackmail. Maybe Mister Raymond isn't aiming to put pressure on somebody in town — somebody we gotta protect.'

'Naw, I reckon Mister Raymond's smart. He'll be leaving town in the morning.'

Archer smiled. He said:

'That right, Raymond? You aiming to stay long in Lynx Falls?'

Bill Raymond dragged on his cigarette. He forced himself to a calmness he was far from feeling. He kept his voice level.

'Since you're so pressing, I may stay on a day or two.' He directed his speech at Archer. 'I bumped into one of your men, a red-faced guy with cauliflower ears answering to the name of Healey. He was putting the old protection gag on the woman in the florist's shop. I thought you might be interested.'

The Chief laughed.

'Keep your nose clean while you're in town, Raymond. I run the force, not you.'

He slipped Raymond's Luger into his pocket.

'I'll keep this,' he said. 'We don't want you shooting any prominent citizens. You can call at City Hall and collect it — on your way out of Lynx Falls. Come on boys — say goodnight to Miss Peter's private dick.'

The cop with the night-stick made a pass at Raymond, who side-stepped quickly. The cop on the bed tossed his cigarette on the sheets and sneered:

'Careful you don't start a fire, bud!'

Archer and his men went through the door. Raymond knocked the still burning cigarette off the bed and put his foot on it — viciously, as if he had Archer beneath his heel. He went down to the bar and called for a whisky. He tossed it back, said:

'I needed that to take the rotten taste out of my mouth. There's something about Lynx Falls that stinks.'

He went to the call box, put in a nickel, and dialled. A feminine voice answered. He said:

'This is Bill Raymond, Miss Peters. I've decided to take your job!'

3

It was raining heavily next morning. Bill Raymond pushed the remains of his breakfast away from him and lit a cigarette. Through the dingy windows of the hotel dining room, Lynx Falls looked even more depressing than it had the day before. The gutters were awash; the sooty trees hung limp, leafless branches under the deluge; a few pedestrians in slickers dodged the spray from the tyres of passing cars.

Raymond leafed through the *Gazette*. It was the typical news-sheet of a small, mid-western town, complete with Births, Marriages, Deaths, and write-ups of polite social parties. Only Lynx Falls was rather more prone to violence than other small towns.

The front page ran a story on a jewel robbery. Mrs. Parkinson's home had been raided and jewels to the value of twenty thousand dollars stolen. A servant had been shot down and killed during the raid. Archer was quoted as having said: 'An arrest is likely in the course of a few days.'

Jerry Goodrich had written a scathing editorial on Archer's comment. He used the incident to point out the lawlessness that ran unchecked in the town; he suggested that a new Chief of Police would be needed before an arrest was made. It was a red-hot editorial, designed to rouse the citizens of Lynx Falls into demanding immediate action. Archer wasn't going to like it.

Raymond left the dining room and donned a raincoat and hat. He crossed Main Street to the *Gazette* office. Goodrich smoked his pipe and looked pleased with himself.

'Hello, Raymond,' he said. 'Dot 'phoned me you'd taken the job. Rely on the *Gazette* to back your play. What are you going to do?'

'What's the most likely place to pick up information in this town? Somewhere the gangs gather to drink and talk.'

'You want O'Connor's place, on Grant,

south side of Columbus Avenue. He runs a pool room with a bar. Most of the gangs use it — including Archer's cops. I doubt if you'll find an honest man there.'

Raymond nodded.

'Sounds just the place. I'll take a run over and buy myself a bottle. With all this rain, the rats will be under cover. Maybe I'll hear a few things to give me an idea. I'm looking for something to set the ball rolling — a piece of dirt I can throw at someone to set the others on his heels.'

'Watch yourself,' Goodrich said. 'By now, you're too well known to play the innocent bystander. I don't want to be writing your obituary just yet.'

Raymond grinned.

'That applies to you too. Archer isn't going to like you after this morning's editorial. Why not lay off till I get something definite on him? Then you can go to town with it.'

Jerry Goodrich scowled over the top of his pipe.

'I hate the idea of laying down to Archer. I feel like ripping into him with everything I've got — it's about time he got some publicity.'

'Sure, I know how you feel. But the *Gazette* may be able to play an important part in stirring up public opinion, later on. And that will be difficult if you're pushing up flowers in the cemetery and Archer has one of his stooges running the paper.'

'Yeah.' Goodrich thought it over. 'All right, I'll go easy till you say it's all right to use the big guns. And will I have a swell time then!'

Raymond went out into the rain. He collected his car and drove south. Beyond Central Plaza, the apartment blocks were gloomier than ever, concrete slabs jammed together between factory chimneys. Even the rain was smoke-laden.

Grant Street right-angled off to the left on Main. Raymond drove slowly past shops with grimy windows, a rusted iron fence bordering a disused warehouse, a laundry that looked as if the wash would come out dirtier than it went in. O'Connor's was next to the laundry, a boarded front with an open door and a sign:

O'CONNOR'S POOL ROOM

Raymond parked his car and walked through the rain. He shook water off his hat as he went through the open door. Inside, brilliant cones of light played over the billiard tables. He moved between the tables, to the bar at the back of the hall.

'Whisky,' he said to the barman.

He sipped the stuff, leaning on the bar and looking round. He was disappointed. O'Connor's wasn't doing much business; two lean men with poker faces played pool at one table; three more threw dice on the bar counter. No one said anything to Raymond.

The barman went through a curtained doorway for a moment. He came back almost immediately. Raymond said:

'I'll take a bottle of Scotch. I hear you have the best stuff in town.'

The barman put a bottle on the counter and changed Raymond's ten dollar bill. He never said a word. A man came in from the street, cursing the rain. He joined the dice throwers, ignoring Raymond after a first searching look.

Bill Raymond lit a cigarette and edged towards the dice players. He said, casually:

'I'm in the market for jewelry if it's going cheap.'

They ignored him, went on throwing the bones. After a while, one man turned his head, and grunted:

'Beat it, copper.'

Raymond smoked in silence. News travelled fast in Lynx Falls; he didn't think he was going to get much out of the inhabitants of O'Connor's pool room. A cop came in, wearing a hat. He didn't bother to take it off, but selected a cue and practised shots on an empty table. Raymond wondered if Archer was having him watched.

Two men pushed past the curtain behind the bar. They came round the counter, up to Raymond. They looked him over carefully. The first man said:

'I'm O'Connor. You want something here?'

Raymond studdied O'Connor. He saw a large man with plenty of meat on his bones. His muscles were flabby from want of exercise, but he still looked tough enough to act as chucker-out. He wore slacks and a sweater over a check shirt. He had a habit of kneading his hands together and cracking the joints of his fingers. It made an unpleasant sound

'Just drinking,' Raymond returned. 'You stock good whisky, O'Connor.'

The large man said: 'Well, drink up and get out. You're not wanted here.'

Raymond smiled thinly.

'You're the third person to say that,' he commented. 'I'm beginning to think I've lost my charm.'

'Outside,' said the second man tersely.

He was so short he might have been a boy. He wore a dark suit with an exaggerated drape; the bulge of a shoulder holster showed he was carrying a gun for O'Connor. He had a patch over his left eye; the other eye stared balefully at Raymond.

O'Connor cracked his knuckles and said:

'You can walk, or you can be carried.'

He nodded at the gunman.

'Hawkeye would prefer that you be

41

carried. You want to argue it with him?'

Raymond looked at Hawkeye and wished Archer hadn't taken his gun. He picked up the whisky bottle by the neck. The cop wearing a hat came over.

'This lug bothering you, O'Connor?' he grunted.

Hawkeye brought out his gun. It was a .38 revolver. He pointed it at Raymond, and said to the cop:

'Stick around. You can testify this snoop was accidently shot after he started a fight.'

Raymond decided he didn't like the frame. He slammed down the whisky bottle on Hawkeye's gunhand and moved for the door. He reached it by the time the gunman had recovered his revolver. A slug buried itself in the door frame; Hawkeye wasn't so good with his left hand.

Raymond made his car through the rain and drove out of Grant Street. He breathed easier to be out in the open, but he regretted smashing the whisky bottle. He hoped Hawkeye's wrist was broken.

From now on, he'd have to watch his

step. The Lynx Falls' gangs had him measured for a wooden box; things were due to happen. Raymond thought it wouldn't take much to start trouble in town. All it wanted was a spark to set off the powder trail; Mrs. Parkinson's jewels reminded him about Smitty, the fence.

Columbus Avenue didn't look quite so despondent, despite the rain. The shops were larger, the prices higher. It was Lynx Falls' Fifth Avenue. Smitty's pawnshop was wedged between a chain store and a soda fountain, a side door with one tiny window displaying jewelled trinkets behind a wire cage. Raymond went through the side door into the shop.

The door tinkled a bell, bringing Smitty from the room behind the shop. He was thin, with sparse hair and a grey face, and looked as if all the blood had been drained out of him. His clothes were neat and well-kept.

'Yes, sir? Can I get you something?'

His voice was smooth, polished like the trays of rings behind the counter. His eyes were bright and fixed on Raymond's face.

'I'd like to look at some engagement

rings,' Raymond said, smiling at the fence.

Smitty showed him two trays and Raymond looked them over.

'I rather like this one with the three diamonds. I'll have to bring the girl in before I decide, of course.'

'Lynx Falls' girl?' Smitty asked casually.

'Miss Peters.'

Smitty's bright eyes sharpened. The name made him regard Raymond with suspicion. Raymond pretended not to notice; he rambled on:

'A little bird told me you might be able to let me have some jewelry cheap. I'm not interested in its pedigree, just the price. I believe Mrs. Parkinson — '

Smitty removed the trays. He snapped:

'Get out! You've got nothing on me — snoop!'

Raymond lit a cigarette and stared at Smitty. He blew smoke in his face and waited. Smitty didn't look the tough sort; Raymond thought he might break under pressure. He leaned on the counter and shoved his face close to the fence's.

'Whoever raided the Parkinson's house

would bring the stuff here because there's nowhere else to sell it in town. Now, start talking before I crack down on you!'

Smitty backed away. His face paled a little; he didn't like this lean young man with the build of a panther. He fumbled for a gun under the counter. Raymond let him get it, then took it away from him.

The street door opened behind him and a voice said:

'Drop it! Archer wants to talk to you.'

It was another cop. This one was hatless and looked like a refugee from Alcatraz. Raymond turned round, but kept hold of Smitty's gun.

'That's fine,' he drawled. 'I'm ready to talk to your chief myself.'

'He threatened me,' Smitty said. 'With my own gun. I want him arrested.'

The cop grunted: 'That's for Archer to decide.'

Raymond went out with the cop into the rain. He felt certain, now, that Archer had been having him tailed. He drove along Columbus to Central Plaza and City Hall, with the cop beside him. They went into the smoke-grimed building, through a door marked:

CHIEF OF POLICE — PRIVATE

Healey was with Archer when Raymond arrived. The red-faced cop with cauliflower ears and a flattened nose scowled. Raymond ignored him, spoke directly at Archer.

'I'm thinking of setting up shop in Lynx Falls. I should do a good trade in brass polish!'

Healey flushed. He didn't like that crack about his dirty buttons. Archer grinned and wiped the brown stain from his chin; he stuck the cheroot back in his mouth and waved Raymond to a seat.

'Just a friendly chat,' he said airily. 'You seem to be heading for trouble in this town. It would be a good idea if you went back east.'

Raymond said: 'You think you may get a hornet's nest about your ears if I'm knocked off in Lynx Falls. You wouldn't want any of my friends investigating your little set-up. So you figure to chase me back home.'

Archer's fat jaws champed on the cheroot. His voice squeaked like a rusty hinge.

'You're not dumb, Raymond. Work it out for yourself — either you leave without trouble, or Miss Peters will have to pay for your funeral. Which is it going to be?'

Bill Raymond shook his head.

'Neither. I've a proposition to put to you — one that'll interest you, I think.'

Archer's beady eyes stared at him from under rolls of fat.

'Shoot,' he said.

Raymond nodded at Healey.

'This is a private arrangement.'

Archer waved a podgy hand at the red-faced cop.

'Take a powder, Healey. You heard him.'

Healey didn't like it, but Archer was the boss. He left the chief's office. Archer grinned at Raymond. He said:

'I wondered if you'd play it our way. I've yet to meet a private dick who didn't want to deal himself in on a juicy racket.

Well, what's your proposition? It had better be good.'

Bill Raymond leaned forward, dragging on a cigarette.

'You and Traill are set to clean up — if one of you can get rid of the other. I figure you're meaning to put him out of the way, but Traill has a lot of backing. Suppose I help you get Traill where you want him?'

Raymond paused to see how Archer was taking it. The chief grunted: 'Keep talking.'

'Mrs. Parkinson's jewels,' Raymond said. 'Maybe you know who took them, maybe not. It's certain that Smitty has them now. He acted scared when I put pressure on him. I figure that if you brought him in and used a little third degree, he'd talk.'

Archer puffed at his cheroot, watching Raymond closely. He stirred his bulk in the chair behind the desk.

'And what would he say?' he asked softly.

'That Nick Traill pulled the robbery, that he brought the jewelry to Smitty.'

Archer shook his head.

'Smitty would be too scared of Nick to talk that way.'

Bill Raymond smiled.

'Would he? If you knocked him around a little, told him he'd get protection from Traill's mob — and that I saw Nick go into his pawnshop with the jewels and pass them over. I figure he'd say what he was told to say then.'

'You willing to sign a statement, to go into court against Traill?' the chief asked carefully.

'Is that necessary? I thought you only wanted to get him in a corner.'

Archer laughed. He got up and waddled to and fro the office, a fat penguin with a cheroot in its mouth. He laughed again.

'It's worth trying,' he said. 'If I can get Nick in jail, he won't stay there long. Easiest thing in Lynx Falls to arrange a prison break — and if Nick gets shot on the way out, no-one will shed any tears.'

He rubbed his podgy hands, smiling. He stopped smiling and said:

'The trouble will be to pick up Nick alone. He rarely travels anywhere without his right-hand gun, Verd — and if he smells trouble, he'll have all his mob with him.'

Raymond considered that angle.

'I figure he'll come alone to meet Miss Peters. Leave me to fix that. I'll deliver him to you, alone, to-night. Have your men waiting to pick him up on the road from his gambling joint.'

'Yeah,' Archer said, 'that's nice. I like that.'

Raymond stubbed out his cigarette and stood up.

'In case of trouble,' he said casually, 'give me back my Luger. Maybe I'll save you the trouble of staging a jail-break.'

Archer studdied him a moment. He seemed satisfied because he grinned and pulled out the desk drawer. He laid the Luger on the desk top.

'Don't shoot anyone else, Raymond,' he warned. 'That wouldn't be healthy.'

Bill Raymond checked the gun and slipped it in his pocket. He felt a lot better to have it. He nodded a goodbye at the chief and left the City Hall. Outside, it was still raining.

The opening gambit had been made.

4

Nick Traill's roadhouse was south of Lynx
Falls, on the road leading to the lake. It
was a large affair of timber and stucco,
with a veranda and balcony. Bill Raymond parked his Cadillac in the shadows
of a group of plane trees and listened to
the dance band swing out a hot number.

The wide doors were glass panelled
and he could see through into the dance
hall. It was nine o'clock and the
roadhouse was doing nice business.
Raymond went in. Back of the floor, a
long bar glistened chromium and plastic.
Raymond called for a whisky, drank it
slowly, and looked about him.

Through an archway the dining room
was crowded with night-clubbers eating,
talking, and drinking. A staircase led up
to another floor. There was a tough
looking guy on duty at the bottom of the
stairs; he carefully vetted everyone who
went up. Raymond guessed the gambling

tables were up there.

He spoke to the barman.

'Nick around? I've a message for him.'

'Yeah?'

Raymond lit a cigarette and enjoyed the flavour. He idly watched the dancers, glancing past them to the stairway.

'Yeah. Tell him Bill Raymond has a message for him. From Dorothy Peters.'

The barman came to life when Raymond mentioned Miss Peters' name. He picked up a house 'phone and spoke into it. He listened, put down the 'phone, and said:

'Okay. Someone will collect you in a minute.'

Raymond watched the staircase. He saw a thin man come down from the upper floor; he had a cleft chin with a narrow slit for a mouth. His eyes were cold and hard and blue. His dark suit had padded shoulders, but the bulge of a gun was just visible for a man with sharp eyes. Raymond didn't miss it. He guessed the thin man was Verd, Traill's right-hand gun.

Verd came across to Raymond. He said, flatly:

'Upstairs, bud, and be good. The boss

wants to see you.'

Raymond smiled at him. They went past the tough guy guarding the stairs and climbed upwards. A balcony led to a long room where a crowd played the tables. They passed through the room to a curtained alcove. Raymond had time to notice that the croupiers were drawing in a lot more money than they paid out.

There was a door behind the curtain. Verd opened it and Raymond entered Traill's private office. The gambler wasn't alone; he had a woman with him. Raymond looked her over and decided she couldn't be anyone other than Elsa.

She was a blonde, twenty-eight or nine, with a lot of powder trying to cover the deepening lines in her skin. She used a vivid red lipstick and some of it had been transferred to Traill's swarthy face. She was tall and well built, and dressed to show it in a tight-fitting gown of red silk with a long, vee neckline. She was sitting back in an easy chair with her legs crossed, nice legs clad in sheer silk hose.

Trail watched Raymond closely, fingering his scar.

He said: 'What's the message, Raymond?'

Raymond handed a sealed note to the gambler. He watched him open it, knowing already what was inside:

Nick,

I want to see you to-night. I have a proposal to put to you. Raymond will drive you out.

Dorothy Peters.

Traill read it twice. His eyes lit up and he licked his lips.

'So she's ready to play it my way,' he said, smiling with all his white teeth. 'That's good. I knew she couldn't hold out much longer.'

Elsa didn't like it. She said:

'Don't try ditching me, Nick — I've got too much on you for you to get away with anything.'

Traill laughed. He kissed her casually.

'Elsa, my darling, don't be so suspicious. It's her money I'm after. When I've got what I want, Verd can take care of her. This is the break I've been waiting for

— with the Peters' fortune behind me, I can break Archer in two. I'll run Lynx Falls on my own after that.'

Verd looked at Raymond, his mouth a harsh slit, his blue eyes cold as ice.

'I don't trust this snoop,' he said flatly. 'It may be a trap.'

'What can the girl do?' Traill sneered. 'She's scared — I bet she thinks she's on a good thing, marrying me. Well, I'll show her.'

'Better let me come with you, boss,' Verd urged.

'Or me,' Elsa said. 'I could handle her all right. I'd enjoy slapping down that stuck-up snob. Thinks she's so good and pure — I'd like to get her in *my* house for a few days. Soon knock that high-and-mighty attitude out of her!'

Traill seemed to think that funny.

'Maybe I'll put her in your place after I've finished with her,' he said. 'Some guys in town would think it funny to have old man Peters' daughter to play with.'

'After you've finished with her?' Elsa snapped. 'Remember what you said, Nick — you're only interested in her *money*.'

Verd looked at the ceiling and whistled airily.

'Sure, Elsa,' Traill said soothingly, 'that's what I mean. After I've got my hands on her dough.'

He smiled at a passing thought, without putting it into words. Raymond guessed he wanted something besides Dorothy's money; he had to control his desire to put a slug between Traill's eyes. He resolved that the gambler would never touch Dorothy while he was alive to do anything about it.

Bill Raymond stubbed out his cigarette and spoke directly at Traill, ignoring Elsa and the gunman.

'You coming along, Nick?'

'Yeah, I'll be right with you. Go down to the bar and wait for me — I've a couple of things to do first.'

Raymond left the office, went through the gaming-room and down the stairs. The dance floor was even more crowded by this time and he had to use his shoulders to get to the bar. He downed a whisky and waited for Traill to show up.

He glanced at the clock; nine-thirty-three. He hoped Archer and his men were waiting; if anything went wrong, Dorothy was liable to be in a jam. Raymond had told Jerry Goodrich to stay with her, just in case.

Traill came downstairs alone. Raymond breathed easier; for a moment, he'd been afraid that the gambler would bring along some of his mob. And in a pitched battle with the cops, anything could happen.

'All set?' Raymond asked.

Traill nodded and headed for the door. Raymond followed after him. No need to shoulder a passage through the crowd now; a lane opened up immediately for the gambler. People feared his power. A couple of girls made eyes at him; Traill smiled back but otherwise ignored them.

Outside, moonlight slanted across the road. It was a bright, still night, after the rain. Low clouds scudded across the hills, making fleeting shadows in the moonlight. The air was clear and crisp.

Raymond started the Cadillac and Traill got in beside him. He swung the car on to the road and headed back for Lynx

Falls. Nick Traill didn't speak. He sat rigid in his seat, a swarthy figure with a handsome face and long sideburns; his silence and the scar crossing his high cheekbone gave him a sinister appearance.

Raymond watched the rear mirror. He cursed under his breath when he saw a green coupé swing after them; Verd or someone in Traill's mob was acting as bodyguard. He hoped Archer would be on his toes when the trap was sprung.

The road to Lynx Falls was wide, with grass verges and trees. There weren't many houses this far from town. Raymond didn't travel with his foot on the accelerator; he kept the Cadillac to the centre of the road and his eyes wary. Somehow, he didn't trust Archer.

The trap came halfway to town, on a sharp bend. Raymond saw a police car drawn across the road. He stamped on the brake and swung the wheel hard. The Cadillac nosed up the bank and shuddered to a standstill, knocking Traill sideways. Police came from everywhere, surrounding the car.

Nick Traill swore viciously and went through the door like a rocket. He knew what this was all about. He had a gun in his hand and it spat lead as he tried to get away. Crimson flame stabbed out; gunshots reverberated loudly and the night air smelled of pungent cordite fumes. Raymond hit the floor of the car as lead whistled over his head. He crawled out on to the grass bank, keeping low.

Archer was playing safe; he had twenty men with him, all armed. They had Traill cornered and were waiting for his ammunition to run out. The coupé came up fast. Raymond saw Elsa at the wheel. Verd was beside her, leaning out of the window, firing. He was a good shot; two cops spun round and fell in the dust.

One of Archer's men had a tommy gun. He opened up on the coupé. Verd kept on firing while Elsa swerved, stopped, and reversed. She had the sense to see they couldn't save Traill by shooting it out. The coupé headed back for the roadhouse, to bring up reinforcements.

Traill's gun was empty. Half-a-dozen cops moved in on him; they used gun butts to batter him senseless, then dragged his limp body to Archer's car. Raymond went across to the chief.

'I told you it would be easy,' he said. 'Traill never suspected anything like this.'

Healey was beside Archer. The red-faced cop scowled at Raymond. He grunted:

'That's why Verd was right behind you, I suppose?'

'Don't tell me you're afraid of one man,' Raymond jeered.

'Shut up, Healey,' Archer snapped. He talked round the butt of a cheroot. 'You did a good job, Raymond. I shan't forget it when I take over Lynx Falls. Now, we've more work to do. I left picking up Smitty in case Traill got wind of it and smelt a rat. We'll attend to the fence right away.'

Healey kicked Traill's unconscious body.

'Why not put a slug in him now?' he wanted to know.

Archer laughed and shook his fat head. He was very pleased with himself.

'No, we'll do this officially. Remember,

we're police, not gangsters.' He chuckled at the joke and his rolls of fat quivered. 'We'll take Nick in, alive; arrange a trial with Smitty and Raymond as witnesses. Only he won't get to the court room — some pals of his will stage a jail-brake and he'll be shot in the escape. That'll give us the chance to cut loose on his mob.'

Raymond said: 'That's smart.'

Healey grunted. He didn't like Raymond; he still remembered how the private dick had called his bluff with the florist.

The cops stowed Traill away and the cars sped towards town. Raymond followed in his Cadillac. They went direct to Smitty's shop on Columbus Avenue. They didn't bother to knock.

Two of Archer's men smashed down the door and they poured into the shop. Smitty came out with a gun. He didn't know whether to be pleased or scared when he saw Archer. The uncertainty showed in his grey face. He staggered back as one of the cops twisted his arm and took the gun away. Healey hit him in the mouth with a night-stick. Smitty gagged on a broken tooth.

Archer waved the glowing tip of his cheroot. He said:

'Nick pinched the Parkinson jewels and passed them to you. You're signing a statement to that effect.'

Smitty's voice lost a lot of its polish; it came out ragged as he spat blood on the floor.

'You're crazy! I daren't say anything against Nick — he'd — '

Healey hit him again. Archer said:

'Nick won't hurt you. We've got him outside, unconscious. Raymond swears he saw Traill pass you the jewelry. You'd do well to stick to that story.'

'Yeah,' Healey said. 'Or we'll get tough.'

He hit Smitty again, just to show him. The fence broke down; he didn't like being hurt.

'All right,' he said. 'I'll say anything you want — but you've got to give me protection from Nick's mob.'

Archer nodded.

'We'll look after you. Now, come on down to City Hall — I have a statement waiting for your signature.'

Smitty went out. Raymond noticed that a load of jewelry had disappeared into the pockets of Archer's cops; the chief wasn't bothered. Archer left a couple of men to search the shop and bring in the Parkinson jewels when they found them. The cars moved away, taking Traill and Smitty to City Hall.

Bill Raymond lit a cigarette and watched them go. He smiled quietly; his night's work wasn't over yet. He drove the Cadillac through back streets to Grant, parked his car outside the laundry. O'Connor's pool room was quiet as he went through the door.

The quiet dropped to a dead hush as Raymond was recognised.

'Christ!' said the barman. 'You've got a nerve, coming back here. Hawkeye's looking for you with a gun in his hand!'

Raymond didn't let it worry him.

'Tell O'Connor I want to see him. Tell him it's important — and to keep Hawkeye out of my way.'

The barman dived through the curtained doorway back of the counter.

O'Connor and Hawkeye came through so fast they might have been waiting on the other side.

O'Connor kneaded his hands so the joints crackled. He seemed surprised to see Raymond. Hawkeye looked viciously at the detective; his right arm was in a sling. He held a .38 revolver in his left hand, pointing it at Raymond. Only O'Connor stopped him using it immediately.

'I guess you know you're practically in the coffin,' O'Connor said, staring at Raymond. 'What decided you to commit suicide?'

Raymond dragged on his cigarette, smiling easily. He hoped the large man could keep Hawkeye under control long enough for him to speak his piece.

'You got a private room? I've news for you — and a proposition. Something you can't afford to ignore.' He paused, then added: 'I'm doing you a favour in coming here, O'Connor.'

The large man was intrigued; he was also impressed by Raymond's nerve in coming back to the pool room after smashing Hawkeye's wrist. He said:

'Spill it!'

Hawkeye snarled: 'Let me take him, boss!'

His one good eye glittered with rage. He wanted to even up the score; he didn't like guys who slugged him with whisky bottles.

Raymond said: 'This is private. You'd better hear me out, O'Connor.'

The large man cracked his knuckles again. He said:

'Okay. But it had better be good. Or you won't be coming out alive.'

O'Connor led the way round the counter, through the curtained doorway. Raymond followed him, smoking a cigarette and trying to look as if he wasn't bothered by the revolver Hawkeye dug in his back.

It was a small room with two chairs and a table. There was a bottle and two glasses on the table. O'Connor sat down and filled the glasses. He passed one to Raymond, and joked:

'The condemned man drank a last whisky!'

Hawkeye leaned against the door, keeping his gun on Raymond. His trigger finger itched; he looked like a small boy with something on his mind — murder.

Raymond emptied his glass. He said:

'Archer's pulled in Nick Traill. Smitty's signed a statement to say that Nick did the Parkinson job. I guess Nick won't be bothered by a trial — Archer's figuring to have him shot in a phony jail-break. Sweet, isn't it?'

O'Connor swore loudly. Hawkeye spat:

'He's lying — it's a trick!'

Raymond chain-lit a fresh cigarette. He turned towards the small gunman.

'Would I stick my neck in here with a story like that if it wasn't true?'

Hawkeye didn't know what to say. O'Connor did.

'Take a gander at City Hall. Find out if Archer has Nick under lock and key.'

Hawkeye went out. O'Connor didn't say anything for a while. He filled Raymond's glass again. Both men drank in silence. Hawkeye was back inside ten minutes. He didn't have to say anything; O'Connor could read the story in his face. The large man lowered his glass slowly, crackling his knuckle joints.

'So, it's true?'

Hawkeye nodded.

Raymond said: 'Well, what about it O'Connor? Archer is starting a big clean-up. He's got Nick, now he's after Traill's mob — when he's wiped them out, it'll be *your* turn. He won't stop till all Lynx Falls is under his thumb.'

The large man swore bitterly. Hawkeye grated:

'The dirty double-crossing swine — I'll fill that bloated hide of Archer's with lead!'

Raymond dragged on his cigarette. He felt a lot more confident now; things were going the way he wanted. He said:

'You don't have a chance on your own. Archer's cops are out gunning for you — and he's the law in this town. Your only chance is to throw in with Nick Traill. Between you, Archer will be outnumbered. The way I figure it is, we pull a real jail-break and get Nick in the clear — then both mobs gang up on Archer.'

O'Connor nodded slowly. His knuckles crackled noisily.

'That's it,' he said. 'That's the way we'll play it.'

Hawkeye was still suspicious. He glared at Raymond.

'What d'you get out of it?' he wanted to know.

Raymond said: 'I want to go on living a bit longer. I was with Nick when he was pulled in — I figure Verd and the boys might think I had something to do with that. I want you to get word to them that I'm on your side, against Archer — that I'll help get Nick out of jail!'

5

'Thank you for the lilies, Mr. Raymond.'

Dorothy Peters smiled a warm greeting to Bill Raymond as he came into the library of her Northwood home. She was looking lovely in a white silk dress that contrasted excitingly with her dark curls and richly carmined lips. Raymond wondered why some men go wild over slim, long-legged glamour girls; Dot's plump curves suited him perfectly.

Jerry Goodrich observed from behind his curved brier pipe:

'Dot doesn't dress up this way for me. Maybe I should have thought to send lilies.'

Raymond grinned at him.

'Maybe if you had blood instead of printer's ink in your veins — '

'Stop it, you two,' Miss Peters scolded. 'Bill, what's the latest progress in the Lynx Falls' clean-up?'

Raymond took the drink Goodrich

handed him and sat down.

'Nick Traill's in prison and Smitty is being held as a material witness. Archer intends to shoot Traill in a fake jail-break. O'Connor plans that the jail-break shan't be a phony — then the two gangs will go after Archer. Whatever happens as a result, Lynx Falls will be short of a few crooks.'

Dorothy said: 'Good!'

Goodrich adjusted his spectacles and watched Raymond's face.

'I don't like the idea of Traill being loose,' he grunted. 'Remember, it was Dot's message that led him into the trap. He's not going to forget that.'

Raymond lit a cigarette, tossed the match into the fire, and inhaled. He blew out a stream of smoke.

'Nick's going to have his hands full taking care of Archer — and I've another wrench to throw in the works.'

Miss Peters leaned forward. 'Yes?' she said eagerly.

Raymond grinned.

'Elsa. Tell me what you know about the blonde.' It was Goodrich who answered.

'Not much,' he admitted, 'beyond the fact that she's Traill's girl friend. I don't see that she's an important cog in the set-up. How do you plan to use her?'

Raymond flicked ash from his cigarette.

'Now tell me about Dr. Fawkes,' he suggested.

Goodrich stabbed the air with the stem of his pipe. He seemed puzzled.

'Fawkes runs spirit seances, all faked of course. He unloads plenty of dough from the rich dames in town. Men too, I believe. He has a side-line in blackmail. What's the connection?'

'To get the sort of information Fawkes requires for his seances, he needs a steady and reliable source. Also for his blackmail racket — I figure Elsa and her girls are in just the position to hand it to him on a plate.'

Raymond waved cigarette smoke in the air. He went on:

'There's another angle. Nick is interested in Dot, as well as her money — '

Goodrich scowled.

'If that filthy dago tries anything, I'll — '

Raymond frowned grimly.

'*I'll* take care of Nick,' he said. 'The point is this; Elsa is jealous — and a jealous woman is dangerous. Maybe I can sell Nick the idea that it was Elsa who framed him with Archer — especially if she is running with Dr. Fawkes.'

Miss Peters laughed.

'I'm glad you're on my side, Bill. I wouldn't like to have you for an enemy — you have a way of stirring up trouble for people you don't like.'

Raymond said: 'That's what you're paying me for.'

He rose to his feet, throwing the cigarette butt in the fire.

'I'm going to run out to the lake and have a chat with Fawkes. Dot, I want you to stay in the house — you'll be safer under cover. And Jerry, keep an eye on her for me, will you?'

Goodrich made a face.

'While you're out buying her lilies, I suppose?'

Raymond grinned. He left the house and went out to his car. He drove back to Lynx Falls and stopped at City Hall.

Archer wiped a brown cheroot stain from his podgy chin as Raymond came.

'Hi, chief,' Raymond said, 'what's new?'

'Verd's getting his boys together. I guess they aim to throw a little lead around — but we'll be ready for them.'

Raymond frowned.

'That puts me in a spot,' he said. 'I guess Verd figures I had something to do with jailing Nick. I'll feel a lot safer when Traill's in a wooden box — his gang won't cut much ice in town when the boss is stretched out in the morgue.'

Archer's fat bulk stirred in the chair. He puffed on his cheroot.

'Then you won't have to worry long. The jailbreak is staged for to-night. Ten o'clock. Nick gets his — then we go after his mob. By morning, I'll have control of Lynx Falls.'

Raymond said: 'That's swell, chief.'

He went back to his Cadillac and drove down Main Street. Verd and O'Connor would know what to do when ten o'clock came — all he had to do was mention the time. Archer was due for a surprise

— and Lynx Falls for a blood bath.

South of Grant Street, the town was even dirtier. Apartment blocks were joined by strings of washing; the gutters were filled with discarded rubbish. The smoke of factory chimneys hung like a grey shroud over sooty trees; shop windows were so grimed that you couldn't see the goods displayed inside.

Further out, the sprawling slums merged into an area of bleak desolation; a no-man's land in the struggle between town and country. Nature won the fight. Raymond hit a green belt, drove along the winding road to the lake, between rows of trees. The hills in the distance were verdant green under the sun.

He passed the sharp bend where Nick Traill had been trapped the night before. He came to the roadhouse; it was a silent building of wood and stucco. No dance band played now; there was no sign of life on the veranda. Only the broad leaves of the plane trees moved in the breeze. Raymond wondered if Verd was inside, planning to rescue his boss. He didn't stop to find out.

The road swung in a long curve, passing between sand hills. It dipped towards the River Lynx and bordered the lake. The water sparkled in the bright sunlight and a fisherman cast his line. Raymond wished him luck as he passed.

Below the lake, the falls that gave the town its name rumbled like distant thunder. Spray drifted across the road, misting the car's windscreen. Hills sprang up sharply beyond the falls and Dr. Fawkes' house nestled amongst the foothills.

It was a modern house, with wide French windows and a flat roof. The walls were pale cream and the rails polished chromium. It looked as phony as the seances that went on under the roof.

Bill Raymond noted the green coupé standing in the drive and wondered if Elsa were visiting Fawkes. There was one obvious way to find out. He went up the steps to the front porch and rang its bell.

The Japanese house-boy came up to Raymond's shoulders. He was dressed in a white linen suit and showed a perfect set of teeth as he smiled. His American was better than Raymond's.

'Yes sir? Whom did you wish to see?'

Raymond smiled back and leaned on the door so the Jap couldn't shut it in his face.

'Dr. Fawkes,' he said. 'My name's Bill Raymond — I'm a friend of Elsa's.'

The Jap went away and Raymond looked round the hall. Cream and chromium seemed to be Fawkes' trademark. The furnishings were expensive; blackmail payed off in Lynx Falls. The house-boy returned.

'Please follow me, sir,' he smiled.

The carpet along the passage was a couple of inches thick. It muffled all footsteps. The Jap showed Raymond through a door at the end of the passage, and withdrew. Raymond studied the three persons in the room.

Elsa, he knew. She said:

'You're no friend of mine, Raymond.'

The bluff, hearty man in tweeds left his chair to greet Raymond. His voice boomed loudly.

'I'm Dr. Fawkes.'

He was nearly bald on top and his

complexion was ruddy. His eyes twinkled merrily; he was a caricature of the life-and-soul of the party.

'This is Underhill,' Fawkes boomed, gesturing to the third person in the room.

Raymond remembered the name; Underhill was Dot's lawyer, another of the big time crooks in Lynx Falls. He was thin, with sharp, angular features, like a man gone sour. Pince-nez spectacles perched on his bony nose and a thin gold chain ran down from them to the breast pocket of his suit. He was neatly dressed and his manner precise.

Underhill pressed the tips of long white fingers together and said:

'I've been waiting to meet you, Raymond. You've been stirring up trouble, and that's liable to be unhealthy — for you.'

Raymond shook his head.

'I didn't start anything. Archer and Traill were after each other's blood before I arrived in town. I got caught in the draught, that's all.'

'That's all, is it?' Elsa jerked out. She sat up, glaring at Raymond. 'You fixed Nick with Archer, you lousy snoop. Well,

Verd will take care of you — '

Raymond put on an injured expression.

'I didn't know anything about that,' he said. 'It was just bad luck for me that I was with Nick when Archer set the trap.'

Underhill said, carefully: 'That isn't the way Archer tells it. He says, you agreed to go witness against Nick, that you led him into the trap.'

Raymond thought quickly. Archer and the lawyer must be working together; that was something he hadn't reckoned on. He said:

'Archer's a liar. He wanted Nick out of the way, meaning to run the rest of you out of town. He's got a power complex, wants to run Lynx Falls on his own. He's double-crossing you, Underhill.'

Dr. Fawkes laughed jovially. He seemed to think it a jolly little party. His eyes twinkled and his hearty voice boomed:

'I'm sure you didn't come here to start a fight, Raymond. What *did* you come for?'

'Yeah,' Elsa snapped. 'Who's next to be delivered to our fat Chief of Police?'

Raymond lit a cigarette. He kept them waiting, studying their faces. Elsa hated him because she thought he'd put Nick away; O'Connor couldn't have got his message to her yet. Dr. Fawkes was curious; he wanted to know why Raymond had called. Underhill was aloof; he had a sharp brain under his skull and he was playing his own game — Archer was just a pawn to him.

'I figured I might have some information to sell, Fawkes,' Raymond said. 'I hear you pay well for the right sort of information — the sort of thing people prefer not to have broadcast.' He stopped, looked at Elsa and the lawyer. It occurred to him that Underhill was in a nice position to pass on some juicy tit-bits to the blackmailer. 'Or am I cutting in on somebody's territory?'

Elsa said: 'I'll love it when Verd fills you with lead!'

Underhill didn't speak; he pressed his fingertips together and regarded Raymond through his pince-nez. Fawkes boomed:

'I see what you mean. A private dick has a way of getting to know things. Well, I'm a business man — what have you got to sell?'

Raymond shrugged. He dragged on his cigarette.

'Nothing yet. I just thought I'd see if you were receptive. Maybe I can get something on Dorothy Peters — how would you like that?'

Underhill showed interest.

'That would be worth a lot of money,' the lawyer commented. 'I think Fawkes would pay well for that. I might add a little extra myself.'

Raymond smiled. Underhill was ready to scoop the pool. He seemed to have both Archer and Fawkes under his thumb; he wanted Traill out of the way. And if he could get a hold over Miss Peters' fortune, he was right on top of the heap. Raymond thought he'd have to put the skids under the lawyer, and soon.

'Don't trust him,' Elsa advised. 'Nick trusted him — and look what happened.'

Dr. Fawkes laughed noisily. Underhill said:

'I can take care of Raymond — or anyone else who double-crosses me.'

The blonde got up. She ignored Raymond, said to Fawkes:

'I'm heading back for town. I'll let you

have the stuff you want as soon as I get it.'

She swayed across the room, out through the door. Raymond stubbed out his cigarette, nodded to Underhill. He said:

'I've some business too. See you again — when I get something on Miss Peters.'

He hurried after the blonde. She was getting into the green coupé when Raymond caught up with her.

'Listen Elsa,' he said quickly. 'I'm on your side — I'm helping O'Connor get Nick out of jail. I've news for you. Tell Verd and O'Connor that the chief has planned the jail-break for ten o'clock to-night. They'd better be early if they want to help Nick.'

Elsa stared at him, uncertain.

'Ten o'clock. That had better be right — or I'll come gunning for you myself. I'm fond of Nick. God help you if anything happens to him.

'Nothing will,' Raymond said, 'if you pass on my message.'

As she drove off, he added, under his breath: '*Yet*!'

6

A clock struck nine. Bill Raymond drew back the curtain and looked through the window. A slight mist drifted across Central Plaza, but he could see the smoke-grimed building of City Hall, and the prison next to it. There weren't many people on Main Street.

Down the road, almost opposite City Hall, was Elsa's house. Raymond thought she had a nerve carrying on right under the noses of the police. Men drifted into Elsa's house, in one's and two's. The men going into the house were mobsters from O'Connor's gang. Raymond had already recognized the bootlegger and Hawkeye.

'War is about to break out,' he observed.

Dorothy Peters crowded to the window. Her perfumed hair brushed Raymond's cheek in the darkness and he wished they had been alone in the room. Jerry Goodrich was just behind them, puffing on his curved brier.

'I suppose this is the first time a newspaper man has ever had a grand-stand view of a jail-break,' he said. 'I wish you'd let me write it up, Bill.'

Raymond shook his head.

'Not yet. I want to weaken the opposition before we go to the people with our story. You'll have your scoop, all right — but this isn't the time. When we've broken the power of the crooks running this town you can print all you want. Until then, it's too dangerous.'

Miss Peters said, suddenly:

'What's going to happen to-night, Bill?'

Raymond shrugged.

'That depends. It depends on how Archer plans to fake his side of the jail-break — and how Verd and O'Connor go about making it a success. My guess is that Traill will get away. I shouldn't be at all surprised if a few crooks get bumped off in the process. And Archer will be mad as hell.'

Silence fell across the room. A floor-board creaked as Jerry Goodrich moved away. Raymond stared through the window, watching the pieces take up their position on the board below; he had a feeling of power from the knowledge that he had started the game.

They were standing in the room of an empty house, the property of Dorothy Peters. The house was on Main Street, overlooking Central Plaza. He saw Archer's men in the shadows, waiting for the chief's signal to attack the prison. The attack was scheduled to fail — and Nick Traill would get a bullet in his heart.

Time passed slowly in the darkness of the empty room. More men slipped into Elsa's house. Raymond had guessed that the house would be used to screen the gangs; but where was Verd? So far, he had seen nothing of Traill's right-hand gun.

The clock struck the quarter hour after nine. The mist swirled across Main, making a grey pattern of shadow between the yellow arcs of the street lights. It was quiet, almost deserted on Central Plaza.

He said: 'Two of Verd's men have just gone into Elsa's.'

'Building up their strength for the

attack,' Goodrich commented. 'They're not taking any chances.'

Dorothy leaned near to Raymond. She was eager for the action to start; she wanted to see Lynx Falls freed of the mobsters who ran the town.

'What are they waiting for?' she breathed.

Raymond slipped his arm round her waist. She was soft and warm under his hand and he wanted to kiss her. He drew her closer. She pushed him away.

'Not now, Bill, please. Wait till it's over.'

Raymond released her. Goodrich said: 'Don't mind me!'

More men slipped into Elsa's house; the place must be like a fortress by now, Raymond thought. He wondered if it would liven things up to tip-off Archer; decided against it. Traill was the fat chief's most dangerous rival; Raymond wanted him out in the open, gunning for Archer.

He looked at his watch; the luminous hands glowed in the dark. Nine-twenty-seven. He saw a black saloon car slowly cross Central Plaza; he tensed — this was it.

The car drew level with the prison as the half-hour struck; thirty minutes before Archer's men were due to start the phony jail-break. Verd got out of the saloon; Raymond recognised his cleft chin and cold blue eyes. Verd didn't hurry; he walked towards the prison wall, a small parcel under his arm.

Two men followed him, carrying tommy-guns. Verd placed the package against the wall, hurried back. Seconds ticked by. One of Archer's men spotted him, shouted an alarm — too late . . . a tommy-gun opened up from behind Verd and the cop spun round, nearly chewed in half by a deadly hail of machine-gun slugs.

The bomb exploded. Main Street was filled with dust and flying debris. The prison wall crumbled away and Verd ran for the gap, shouting:

'Nick — this way, Nick!'

Archer ran out from City Hall. He seemed confused; his jail-break wasn't going to schedule and he wanted to know why. He got the idea when machine-gun bullets sprayed in his direction. He dived back, moving remarkably fast for his bulk. He dropped his cheroot and shouted at his men:

'It's Traill's mob. Don't let Nick get away — shoot them down!'

The cops who had been hiding for the ten o'clock job came to life. They opened up on the black saloon; wilted under tommy-gun fire and dived for cover. More of Archer's men came out of City Hall. Main Street was a confusion of mist and smoke, shouting and firing. O'Connor's gang erupted from Elsa's house, taking the cops by surprise. A crossfire of lead slugs raked Central Plaza.

Hawkeye was beside O'Connor, using his .38 left-handed; he still wore his right arm in a sling. The patch over his eye gave him a sinister appearance. O'Connor was using two .45 automatics, firing alternately from each hand. The cops didn't like the way they'd been trapped; they shot back desperately.

Verd came through the gap in the prison wall, helping Nick Traill. Guns covered them as they made for the saloon. Archer screamed:

'Get Nick! Get him, you stupid fools!'

Traill grabbed Verd's gun and aimed at the chief; he badly wanted to even the score for the way Archer had framed him. His shot clipped Archer's ear, made him duck hurriedly. More cops arrived in a station wagon; they had tommy-guns. For several minutes, Lynx Falls reverberated with incessant gunfire. O'Connor's mob started retreating. Verd got Nick into the saloon; the car moved forward, guns chattering from the rear window.

The police gave chase till one of Traill's mob threw a grenade at it. Orange flame flashed; the wagon heeled over, spilling twisted metal and shattered glass on to dead bodies. The petrol tank exploded in a sheet of flame.

When the confusion died away, Main Street was strangely silent. The mist drifted over debris and limp bodies stretched at unnatural angles. Only Archer's men were left milling in Central Plaza; Traill's saloon had got clean away; his gang, and O'Connor's had vanished into the night air.

Dorothy Peter's started counting the dead.

'Seven of Archer's men,' she totalled. 'Four of Traill's; five of O'Connor's gang. That's a nice start, Bill.'

Bill Raymond smiled grimly.

'That should start something in this town,' he said with satisfaction. 'Archer and Traill will be after each other like a couple of wildcats. With a little more stirring from me, this trouble should bring in all the Lynx Fall's mobs — and then we'll clean up.'

She was suddenly worried.

'You'll be careful, Bill? I don't want you getting hurt.'

Raymond took the opportunity to kiss her. Her lips were moist and firm on his. He held her till she gasped for breath.

'I'll be careful,' he promised. 'I'll be coming back for more! Now, I must go and see Archer — don't want him losing heart at this stage of the game.'

'When you two love-birds have quite finished,' Jerry Goodrich said sarcastically, 'perhaps I can get over to the *Gazette* office and set the presses rolling.

The few honest citizens we have left in town will be showing a certain amount of curiosity — they'll want to read all about the fracas in the morning paper.'

'Okay,' Raymond said, 'but take Dot home first. You know the line to take in the *Gazette*? Demand that Archer takes steps to clean up the hoodlums that plague this lovely, unspoilt town. Put plenty of pressure on him — I don't want this quarrel with Nick to end here.'

'Sure, I'll make his blood boil; leave it to me.'

They used the back door. Goodrich and Dorothy Peters drove out to Northwood. Bill Raymond crossed Central to City Hall. He found Archer wiping blood off his ear, chewing on a cheroot, and swearing at his men.

'What happened?' Raymond asked innocently. 'You put on a good show. Nick get his?'

Archer glared at him. His fat body quivered with rage.

'Where in hell have you been, Raymond? Traill's gang shot the guts out of us. Nick got away.'

Raymond pretended surprise.

'Somebody must have tipped Verd off,' he commented.

Healey turned on Raymond. He'd been badly scared and wanted someone to take it out on. He said:

'Maybe it was you. You knew the time and — '

Archer studied Raymond closely.

'Yeah, maybe you changed sides. Never trust a private dick.'

'Me? You're crazy!' Raymond said. 'I helped bait the trap for Nick — and he knows it. You think I want him setting his mob on me?'

Archer's beady eyes stared hard at Raymond. His podgy hands clenched, and relaxed.

'That's right. Nick's gonna be after you too. I guess you wouldn't be dumb enough to turn him loose.'

Raymond smiled. He lit a cigarette, blew a smoke-ring.

'I bet Smitty's shaking in his shoes. The fence is going to regret signing that statement.'

Healey laughed harshly; the red-faced cop sneered:

'Smitty's past worrying. Nick plugged him on the way out.'

That would please Dot, Raymond thought grimly. The first of the big-time crooks had got his: the cleanup had started.

Archer said: 'It's open war now. I've got to get Nick before he gets me — and I will. I've brains and power on my side. Underhill's backing my play.'

Raymond looked doubtful.

'That so?' he drawled. 'I saw him talking with Elsa, this afternoon. I wonder if — '

Archer swore.

'Underhill knew the jail-break was set for ten tonight. If that shyster lawyer has double-crossed me, I'll get him. He thinks he's the bigshot around town — I'll show him who's boss!'

Raymond flicked across the room. He said:

'You're right, chief. Underhill's getting big ideas — I wouldn't trust that guy. He needs taking care of.'

'Maybe you think you can do that?' Healey snorted.

'Maybe.' Raymond dragged on his cigarette. 'Anyway, you can rely on me to back your side, chief. I want Nick out of the way before he gets around to me.'

'Traill isn't going to last long,' Archer said viciously. 'As soon as I've got the boys together, I'm going after him. I can pin murder on him now. Tomorrow, I'll bust him wide open.'

Raymond nodded.

'I'll be around,' he said, and went out.

The mist was thicker now. Raymond picked up his Cadillac and drove along Main Street, heading south. He thought it would be a good idea to talk to Nick Traill and foster a little more ill-feeling. Nothing like striking while the iron was hot.

The headlights of his car cut a swathe through the night mist. He left Lynx Falls behind, drove across the open country-side to Traill's roadhouse. Downstairs was in darkness; the place was closed for business. Lights from the upper floor told him that Nick was home.

Raymond parked his car under the plane trees and knocked on the door. A husky voice said:

'Who is it?'

'Bill Raymond. I want to see Nick.'

A flashlight stabbed the darkness. Behind the circle of light, Raymond saw the muzzle of an automatic.

'Come on in,' invited the husky voice. 'Nick wants to see you, too.'

Raymond went in. The gunman was right behind him as he went upstairs. The gambling room was full of mobsters, O'Connor's as well as Traill's. In Nick's private office, Raymond found the gambler and Verd, O'Connor and Hawkeye. Elsa was absent.

Traill looked as if he'd taken a beating. The scar down his face had opened up and dried blood caked his swarthy face. He was missing a couple of front teeth.

'Looks like you didn't enjoy your stay at City Hall,' Raymond commented.

Traill began cursing. He used a lot of foul words to describe the Chief of Police. When he'd cooled off, he said:

'They tied my hands, then set Healey

on me with a night-stick. I'm gonna get that lousy copper one day. Archer stood over me and jeered while I took a beating — the fat, bloated swine!'

'Yeah, I don't like that guy either,' Raymond said. 'He tried to run me out of town — and that's something I don't stand for.'

Verd showed impatience. The man with the cleft chin brought out a gun and pointed it at Raymond.

'This snoop framed you, boss. What's the use of wasting time? Let me finish him.'

Raymond laughed.

'Your brain is addled — would I walk in here of my own free will if I had framed Nick? I tipped off you and O'Connor, through Elsa, to the time of the phony jail-break. I'm on Nick's side.'

'Yeah?' snarled Verd. 'And how do you account for the trap Nick walked into? You brought the message from the Peters' dame. You were with Nick when he was cornered.'

'You've got some explaining to do,' Nick Traill said. 'Sure, you helped me get out — I've had the story from O'Connor — and I'm obliged to you, Raymond. But somebody framed me. Who?'

Raymond shrugged.

'I don't know. Maybe it was Elsa — she was jealous as hell when you showed interest in Dorothy Peters.'

Verd said: 'You're crazy — Elsa would do anything for the boss.'

Traill seemed to be thinking aloud.

'A jealous woman can be plenty dangerous.'

Raymond decided to push home the point.

'She was out at Fawkes' place, this afternoon. I guess she didn't waste any time once you were inside. Maybe Fawkes put her up to it — he's got a nice racket. Maybe he figures Elsa will be more use to him with you out of the way.'

'Yeah,' Traill said softly. He seemed to be thinking hard. 'She sees too much of that blackmailer. I guess I'll take care of him — Elsa too, when I get around to Miss Peters.'

O'Connor cracked his knuckle joints. He said:

'Your domestic troubles will have to wait, Nick. We've got to deal with Archer first. We've got to stick together till that fat slob's stiff and cold.'

'That's sense,' Hawkeye added.

Verd glared at Hawkeye; there wasn't much love between the two gunmen. They hated the idea of working together.

'Archer says he'll be gunning for you tomorrow night,' Raymond remarked. 'He won't have licked his boys back into shape before then.'

Traill nodded.

'We'll be waiting for him.'

O'Connor laughed.

'With tommy-guns!'

Raymond moved for the door. He waved a hand casually.

'Be seeing you, Nick. If I learn anything of the chief's plans, I'll tip you off.'

Traill said: 'Do that.'

Raymond smiled at Verd and left the room. He went downstairs, out into the shadows. The night air was cold and damp; the mist lay heavily on the countryside and the moon was blotted out. He started the Cadillac and headed back for town.

Bill Raymond whistled as he drove. His campaign was shaping nicely; Archer was engaged in open warfare with Traill and O'Connor; Nick was suspicious of Elsa and Dr. Fawkes; Archer had the idea it was Underhill who had doublecrossed him; Smitty was dead. The Lynx Falls' mobs were at each other's throats and blood was due to flow.

Maybe he'd call on Fawkes again, and sow a little discontent between the blackmailer and Underhill. But there was one combination he had to break up fast — Nick Traill and O'Connor. Together, they were a powerful force for evil; Raymond decided to do something about that right away.

Reaching Lynx Falls, he drove up Main Street, stopped outside Elsa's house. The blonde opened the door herself; she seemed to be alone.

'Nick's okay,' Raymond said, 'I just left him. But you want to watch O'Connor — he's selling Nick the idea that you framed him with Archer, to leave him and join Fawkes. That O'Connor's trying to bust things up so he gets control of the town himself.'

Elsa laughed.

'Nick knows me better than that. He'll soon shut O'Connor's mouth.'

'Maybe,' Raymond said thinly, 'I just thought I'd mention it. It struck me that O'Connor meant business — and you wouldn't want anything to come between you and Nick. Not with Dorothy Peters on Nick's horizon.'

'I'll fix O'Connor good!' The blonde said it as if she meant it; Raymond thought she did.

He went back to his car, smiling. Elsa would go to work on the bootlegger and the Trail-O'Connor combination would go up in gun-smoke.

Raymond drove up Main Street to the Palace Hotel. He wanted a meal and some sleep. Across the road, the presses behind the *Gazette* office were rolling, printing the story of Nick Traill's escape; by morning, all Lynx Falls would know that war had been declared between the gangs.

Bill Raymond was smiling broadly as he walked past the pasty-faced clerk, up the stairs to 107; he thought he'd done a good night's work. Dot was going to be pleased when he told her — and that made him happy, too.

He moved the curtain over the window in his room and looked out over Main Street. It was quiet; the quiet before the storm. Tomorrow, the storm was due to break.

7

The wind came from the west, a gentle breeze carrying the scent of pine and sage. Bill Raymond, at the wheel of his Cadillac, enjoyed the morning air. He drove out of Lynx Falls, along Columbus Avenue, into the wind.

Past the rows of shops and beyond the straggling houses forming a suburban ring, the road curved in a long arc. The hills in the distance glinted greenly under the sun's rays and trees moved their leaves in the breeze. Raymond was on his way to call on Underhill; he wanted to know where the lawyer lived and, if he got the chance, to throw another spanner in the workings of the Lynx Falls' mob.

Round the bend, a low iron railing bordered Delaware Park and kids played baseball on the green: opposite, was Underhill's home. It was a weathered, yellow brick house with the walls almost covered by climbing ivy. The roof slanted sharply and the upper windows were joined by a railed balcony. The garden was small and neat with bright flowers in trimmed plots dotting the lawn.

Raymond left his car in the road and walked the short drive to the house. His curiosity was roused by the police car outside the front porch. Maybe Archer was calling on Underhill — but then, why should the Chief of Police park his car behind a shoulder-high hedge of evergreen, so that it was screened from the road? Archer had no need of secrecy in his visits to the lawyer.

Raymond decided to play a hunch; something told him he'd do well to listen in before revealing himself. He ignored the front door and its painted iron knocker; went round the side of the house, keeping off the gravel path and using the grass verge to muffle his footsteps.

At the back, an open French window intrigued him. Voices drifted out. Raymond crept up to the window and peered through. He saw Underhill talking with a uniformed cop, not Archer. He recognized Healey's burly form and red face, his cauliflower ears and flattened nose. He watched, and listened.

Underhill was talking in his neat, precise manner. The lawyer's sour face wore something that would have passed for a smile on anybody else. His eyes gleamed behind the pince-nez and he pressed his fingertips together in a characteristic pose.

'You'll do as I say, Healey,' the lawyer said. 'If you carry out my orders you've nothing to worry about — if you don't, you know what to expect.'

Healey evidently did; he didn't look happy about it.

'Okay,' he grunted. 'I'll do it. You don't have to keep throwing that murder charge in my face — only *you* know the Chicago cops are looking for me. So I bump Archer. Okay.'

Raymond tensed. This sounded promising.

Underhill said: 'It's easy. To-night, Archer will be leading his men in the attack on Traill's roadhouse. In the confusion, you'll have no difficulty in putting a bullet through him. You've some cops you can rely on to back your play; see there's no slip up — then you'll take over the force. With you acting chief, I'll run Lynx Falls the way *I* want it. And when you've burned out Traill and O'Connor, we'll clean up.'

Healey's face lit up.

'Yeah,' he said. 'I've one or two ideas to play on when I'm Chief of Police. One is to settle with that private snoop, Raymond. And — '

'I'll give the orders,' Underhill said calmly. 'You'll carry them out. Got that, Healey?'

The red-faced cop nodded. Underhill fingered the gold chain on his pince-nez. He said:

'I'll teach Archer to doublecross me. That fat slug accused me of tipping off Traill's mob about the time of the jail-break. He insulted me — and he'll die for it.'

'Sure,' Healey growled. 'I'll get him.'

'I've been intending to fix Archer for some time,' the lawyer went on. 'He's been getting above himself. He's forgotten that, without me, he'd never have been chief at all. Now I'll get rid of him and set you up. But don't get any ideas, Healey. You're just my stooge; I pull the wires and you jump to it. If you forget that, I'll replace you too.'

'I'll enjoy being chief,' Healey said. 'There's some old scores I want to pay off.'

'Stick to the programme,' Underhill insisted. 'Archer first — then Traill and O'Connor.'

Raymond decided he'd heard enough. He didn't want to be caught listening. He slipped away, back to his Cadillac, and drove off. Nick Traill would appreciate knowing about Underhill's plan to replace Archer.

The Cadillac swung into Juniper Drive, heading back for Lynx Falls. He drove up Main Street and stopped at a café for lunch. After roast lamb, fruit and coffee, Raymond lit a cigarette and headed for the roadhouse. He noticed that the wind was rising.

The wood and stucco building had an air of desertion about it; the downstairs windows were boarded up; the doors locked. Guns peeped through the upstairs windows and a face showed as Raymond parked his car. It was the only sign of life. Traill was preparing for a siege.

The door opened as Raymond approached. A gun showed, and a voice said:

'Come on in; and snap it up!'

The gangsters were downstairs, drinking at the bar. Raymond got some dirty looks as he preceded Verd upstairs. Traill and O'Connor were alone in the office; Verd went away.

'Drink?' said Nick Traill.

Raymond nodded. He watched the two gang leaders; Traill seemed on edge; O'Connor was in a sulky mood. Raymond wondered if Elsa had been around, poisoning the air. He drank the whisky Traill handed him, sat down, smoking.

'News,' he said briefly.

Nick Traill leaned forward. His long scar was livid; his swarthy face seemed to have lost a little more of its handsomeness since he had been in jail. O'Connor cracked his knuckle-joints and glowered at Raymond; he seemed suspicious.

'Underhill plans to have Archer put out

of the way during to-night's raid. Healey's going to be acting chief, under the lawyer's orders.'

Traill swore softly.

'Healey won't last long once I sight him.'

He thought about it and his face smiled coldly.

'That's an idea,' he said.

O'Connor frowned: 'What is?'

Traill rubbed the side of his aquiline nose.

'I know a boy in the force who'd just love to be acting chief. Maybe there are one or two more who like easy money. I reckon we can split Archer's mob in two and wipe them out.'

He thought about it some more, said:

'It'll be easy.'

The bootlegger showed interest.

'Yeah, with the cops in two halves, we got nothing to worry about. We'll play it that way, Nick.'

Raymond said: 'Elsa been around? She's one girl who's got your welfare at heart, Nick.'

O'Connor spat at the floor.

107

'That crazy bitch — '

'Shut up,' Traill said sharply. 'Leave Elsa out of this, O'Connor — or I'll be seeing you after I get through with Archer.'

The two gang leaders glared at each other. Raymond kept a smile off his face; Elsa seemed to have played it the way he wanted. He got up, moved to the door.

'I'll drop by to-night and see what's cooking, Nick.'

'Sure, I like to have news of the outside world. Keep me posted — but don't get any ideas about changing sides. I don't like doublecrossers — and my gun hand doesn't shake.'

'That goes for me too,' O'Connor added.

Raymond went downstairs, across the hall and out into bright sunlight. He wondered if he'd overplayed his hand: Traill and the bootlegger were getting suspicious. He'd have to watch his step in future.

The Cadillac moved along the road to Lynx Falls. The trees bent and leaves rustled; the wind howled and grew in strength. A gale was blowing up from the west.

Raymond headed for Northwood to pass on his news to Dot — anyway, he wanted to see her again before the night came and terror struck at Lynx Falls.

★   ★   ★

City Hall was the centre of grim activity. Bill Raymond watched the cops arm themselves with tommy-guns and automatics. Archer gave last minute instructions.

'Listen boys, we're going to clean out Traill's roadhouse. O'Connor and Nick are holed up inside. Their boys are armed and they're going to throw a lot of lead around, but don't let that worry you.'

Archer wiped a brown stain from his chin. He stuck the cheroot back in his mouth and talked round it.

'The roadhouse is wood, and there's a strong wind blowing — that's all to the good. We surround the house, keeping under cover. When we're all set, we fire the house. They'll have to come out — or roast.'

The chief paused; his beady eyes were bright with cunning. He gestured with a gun held in a fat hand.

'As they come out, we'll shoot 'em down. It'll be easy — like mowing down sitting ducks. They won't have a chance. The fire behind them, guns in front. Not one of those rats will see tomorrow.'

The cops murmured approval; they weren't keen on a shooting match with two powerful gangs. But the way Archer outlined it, they weren't going to get a scratch. It would be a picnic.

They filed out to the waiting cars, guns loaded and ready for action. Raymond stayed beside the chief. He wanted to be in on this. Out of the corner of his eye, he saw Healey watching Archer. The red-faced cop was looking at his chief as if calculating just how much longer he had to live. There was another policeman eyeing both Archer and Healey.

He was a tall, rangy man with a slight stoop; he had shifty eyes and a hare-lip. A hand-rolled cigarette dangled loosely from his mouth. Raymond guessed he was the cop Nick Traill had bought and intended to instal as acting chief.

They piled into the cars. The chief had picked men with him. Healey had a wagon load of his buddies. The cop with the hare-lip took another wagon; his men had been told what to expect. Raymond followed behind the convoy in his Cadillac.

The cars moved south down Main Street, travelling fast. It was nearly eleven and the streets were deserted. A pale moon cast faint beams over the country-side as the convoy left Lynx Falls. The wind from the west rose steadily to gale force. It was going to be a stormy night in more than one way.

Raymond tried to forecast what would happen at the roadhouse. He didn't think Traill had much to worry about — unless it was a shot in the back from O'Connor. Archer was the man who was going to lose out to-night. Raymond wondered who would come out top man, Healey or the cop with the hare-lip.

The cars stopped a little way from the roadhouse and Archer led his men forward on foot. Some of the cops carried petrol drums; others, grenades and tommy-guns. Raymond kept in the rear, his fingers tight round the butt of the Luger in his pocket. He thought he might have to do a little shooting himself.

They approached the roadhouse cautiously. Traill and O'Connor would be expecting an attack and there was no point in walking into a trap. Archer signalled his men to spread out, to surround the house; he didn't want anyone to escape.

The wind was cold and the plane trees bent under its driving force. The roadhouse was a gaunt silhouette against the dark hills and the grass was pale under ghostly moonlight. Clouds, dark and threatening, scurried across the night sky.

Raymond studied the silent building. The doors and windows downstairs were boarded up; no light showed anywhere. Upstairs, on the balcony, he thought he detected a movement. A gun, perhaps. Archer moved round to the back of the house; his men carried the petrol drums. Raymond dropped back into the shadows, following.

He heard Archer's voice, a squeaky whisper blown back by the gale:

'Let them go — now!'

The drums had been punctured so the petrol leaked out. Two cops pushed them down the slight incline; the drums rolled towards the house, leaving a smelly trail of liquid. They bumped against the timber wall, and stopped.

Archer shouted: 'Come out, Traill — I'm waiting for you!'

Rifle fire broke out from the balcony of the roadhouse. Red flame spurted through the darkness; puffs of smoke billowed and vanished in the wind; sharp whiplash cracks split the silence. It was a bad night for accurate shooting; the gale carried the bullets wide of Archer by twenty feet. One slug furrowed the earth in front of Raymond.

The cops started firing back. They emptied machine-gun magazines into the timber wall. The mobsters inside opened up in earnest and the night air was filled with noise and flame.

Raymond dropped back behind a mound, to watch from cover. Archer's voice came to him again:

'The petrol . . . fire it!'

A cop drew the pin from a grenade. He didn't get the chance to throw it. Healey came up from behind, an automatic in his hand. His face glowed with sadistic pleasure. He fired once — the cop spun round, and dropped. The grenade went off under him, blowing his body to pieces.

Healey went up to Archer and jabbed the automatic in the chief's stomach.

'This is it, you fat slob,' he grunted, and jerked the trigger three times.

Archer's podgy face paled. His fat body jerked in agony and he clutched at his middle with soft white hands. He moaned as he sank to the ground. Healey kicked him in the face.

'Take your time dying,' he jeered. 'There's no hurry!'

Healey thought he had it all his own way now. He shouted:

'Traill's got the chief! Don't let any of the rats get away!'

Healey fancied himself in the role of acting chief; with Underhill backing his play, he thought he was on a good thing.

But first he had to get rid of Traill and O'Connor. He shoved his gun back in its holster and grabbed a hand grenade. He pulled out the pin and swung back his arm to throw it at the petrol drums.

The tall cop with the hare-lip had other ideas. He, too, liked the notion of playing acting Chief of Police — with Nick Traill supporting him. He had a submachine-gun cradled in the crook of his right arm. He fixed Healey in the sights and cut loose with a hail of lead.

The red-faced cop who liked threatening old ladies got it in the chest — a stream of heavy slugs that ripped his lungs apart and left him coughing blood. The grenade rolled from his hand as he writhed in death-agonies. The bomb went off, throwing steel splinters in his face. Healey lay quite still after that.

Hare-lip shouted orders at his men. They opened up on the cops who had been supporting Archer and Healey. Traill and O'Connor's mobs were firing from the upstairs window of the roadhouse. The cops couldn't make it out; they were being shot at from the ground as well as the house; they assumed some of Traill's men had sneaked out to take them from the rear. It was a night of confusion with most of them not knowing friend from foe; they shot at anything that moved.

Raymond, watching from cover, decided that Traill was getting things too much his own way; he wanted to even the fight, to give both parties the chance to wipe out more thugs on each side. He crawled forward and picked up a grenade. He looked around; no-one had seen him — they were all too busy keeping alive and shooting the next man.

Raymond withdrew the firing pin and threw the grenade; the bomb curved through the air and landed beside the petrol drums. The seconds dragged out . . . then a sheet of red flame slashed the darkness. Steel splinters made a shrapnel cloud and the petrol caught light. It blazed into an inferno; black oily clouds were blown on the wind and the wooden walls of the roadhouse burst into flames. The fire mounted quickly in intensity, fanned by the gale.

Mobsters came out of the burning

house like rats from a sinking ship. Those that couldn't make the downstairs door jumped from the balcony. The cops who weren't in Hare-lip's command shot them down as they came out; silhouetted against the raging fire, the gangsters made easy targets.

Tommy-guns chattered viciously; grenades went off almost silently in the noise of the inferno; black smoke billowed across the open fields. It was bright as day in the firelight and the moon's faint beams were lost except on the distant hills.

Sharp jets of crimson flame stabbed out as cops shot it out with mobsters. Archer's plan would have worked — not one of Traill or O'Connor's gangs would have got away alive — if it hadn't been for Hare-lip and his men. Shooting from behind the cops, they gave the hard-pressed mobs the chance they needed.

Traill and Verd, with their men, shot an avenue to the cars; O'Connor, with Hawkeye and the remaining members of the bootlegger's outfit went across country, firing back as they ran.

Nick Traill shouted at Hare-lip as he started a car and drove off:

'Good work, Kirk. I'll see you tomorrow and fix things.'

The shooting died away. Both Traill and O'Connor had escaped. Kirk, the hare-lipped cop, gathered his men and drove back to town. It was strangely silent round the burnt-out shell of the roadhouse, silent as the grave — the grave of Archer and Healey, a dozen more crooked policemen and gangsters.

The west wind howled across the open country, scattering ashes. Raymond came out from cover to survey the scene. He lit a cigarette and smoked it quickly, hardly tasting the weed for the smell of charred wood and dead bodies. He turned away, his stomach muscles tightening.

Archer had lost in his bid for power, and Underhill was due for a shock when he found out Healey was dead too. Traill held Lynx Falls in the palm of his hand, with Kirk to give his reign a semblance of law — there was only O'Connor in his way now. Raymond decided it was time to throw Traill and O'Connor into opposition. Maybe he should go to work on Elsa — or would Underhill be able to resist Traill's power?

There was a call box down the road. Raymond used it to 'phone the lawyer. Underhill's voice came through, clipped and calm:

'Is that you, Healey?'

'No; Bill Raymond speaking. I thought you might be interested in the news. Traill and O'Connor got away.'

Underhill's voice was casual: 'And Archer?'

'Dead. You'll have to find another stooge now.' Raymond paused for effect. 'Healey was acting chief — for about two minutes. Then he bought it.'

Underhill almost jumped down the receiver.

'What! Healey — '

Raymond cut him short: 'Yeah, Healey's dead, too. A hare-lipped cop by the name of Kirk is acting chief now. I guess he's taking Traill's orders. You'll have to watch your step, Underhill!'

He put down the 'phone, smiling,

imagining the lawyer's rage and disappointment. There would be fear in his heart too. Traill wouldn't be taking orders from Underhill.

Bill Raymond left the call box and walked to his car. He stood looking at the night sky; dark clouds hurried by on the west wind, travelling towards Lynx Falls. He spoke aloud:

'Terror rides the west wind . . . '

8

Bill Raymond frowned at the *Gazette* as he finished his breakfast in the dining room of the Palace Hotel. Jerry Goodrich had gone to town with an editorial lashing the crooks who terrorized Lynx Falls.

ANOTHER CROOKED
CHIEF OF POLICE

Since Chief Archer died in the attack on Nick Traill's roadhouse last night, it has become obvious that acting-chief Kirk is just a stooge for Traill. Once more, the town is under mob-law. With pleasure, we announce that more than a dozen gangsters were killed in the fight that ended in Traill's gambling den being razed to the ground. When are the citizens of Lynx Falls going to wake up to the fact that there is only one way to deal with the thugs who spoil our town?

We do mean by fighting these murderous gangs with their own weapons and running them out of town. While Kirk remains head of the police force, Lynx Falls will know no peace. Law and order is a farce in a town where the Chief of Police takes his orders from a man known to be a gambler, a crook, and a murderer . . .

There was a lot more in a similar vein. Goodrich had spread himself over two full columns on the front page. Traill and Kirk and the rest of the Lynx Falls mobs weren't going to like it — they were going to look for the editor with guns in their hands.

Raymond swore briefly. He couldn't understand why Jerry had written such a scathing editorial; it was in direct opposition to his orders. Goodrich would have to sleep with one eye open after this; he wouldn't be safe from the men he had openly indicated in print.

Raymond pushed his breakfast aside. He went through the tiled hall of the hotel and crossed the street to the *Gazette* office. Jerry Goodrich looked up, startled, as he stormed in.

'You damned fool!' Raymond snapped. 'Whatever possessed you to write this stuff? Don't you know you've signed your death warrant? Every gunman in town will be looking for you.'

Goodrich flushed.

'The *Gazette* is my paper,' he said, 'and I'll run it *my* way. I'm tired of hiding behind you — I want to take a crack at the gangs myself. This is my way of doing it. I figure I can rouse the people to action and — '

'You'll rouse somebody,' Raymond returned. 'Traill, and Kirk, and every small-time crook who fancies himself with a gun.' He repeated, with emphasis: 'You damned fool!'

Goodrich puffed on his pipe. He didn't appear worried by Raymond's opinion of his mental processes. He said:

'So far, I've stood down and let you take all the risks, Bill. I reckon it's time I declared my hand. I'm backing you all the way. How do you think I feel, keeping

123

quiet while you walk into danger every day? How do you think I feel, sitting with Dot and knowing she's worrying about whether she'll see you again? Every time I look in her eyes, I want to be right beside you, backing your play. She wants you to come through with a whole skin — it doesn't matter about me — '

Raymond glared at the editor.

'Listen,' he said. 'You're the only man in this town I can trust. Traill's free and he's going to start thinking about Dot. I can't be in two places at once — that's why I want you to stay with her. Somebody's got to protect her.'

Goodrich didn't look happy.

'Sure, I'll watch out for Dot.'

'After you're dead?' Raymond snapped. 'You've got to lie quiet for a bit. Leave the *Gazette* to run itself and give orders to lay off the gangs. *I'll* tell you when it's safe to tear into them. Remember. I'm a professional in the trouble business, you're not.'

Goodrich didn't say anything. Raymond went on:

'I want you to go out to Northwood

and stay with Dot. Don't leave the house and keep her under cover. If you really love Dot, you'll do as I say.'

The editor writhed in his seat. He thought about it.

'Okay, Bill,' he replied at last. 'I'll do it. No more editorials till you give the word. I'll leave for Northwood right away.'

Raymond clapped him on the shoulder.

'Good man, Jerry; I know I can rely on you.' His voice softened. 'I know how you feel — it's always the man who sits around and waits, who has the toughest time. But you'll be doing the right job if you look after Dot.'

They shook hands, and Raymond started out for City Hall. Although the sun shone over Lynx Falls, there were few people on the sidewalks; no-one knew when gang war was going to break out again, and most people kept indoors, out of the way of stray bullets.

Raymond recognized some of Traill's mob hanging round City Hall; they seemed on good terms with the uniformed cops. He saw none of O'Connor's gang. Raymond went up the steps, along a passage to the room marked Chief of Police.

Inside, he found Kirk and Elsa. They stopped talking as he entered. Raymond had wondered how Traill got word to Kirk; now he knew. The blonde was acting as messenger.

'Nick around?' he asked.

Elsa snapped: 'Why, would you care?'

Raymond looked pained.

'Nick's a friend of mine. I helped get him out of jail, didn't I? I passed the word about Underhill casting Healey for acting chief. I just like to know where my friends are — I guess he won't be using the roadhouse after last night — and I thought you could tell me.'

Elsa wore a green skirt and a tight-fitting blouse of white satin. Her artificial blonde hair draggled down past her shoulders and she smelled of cheap powder and perfume. Her vivid red lipstick had been put on crooked. Raymond guessed she wasn't usually up and about so early in the morning. She was sitting on a chair in front of Kirk's desk.

She said: 'Maybe I could tell you — but I shan't. I don't like you, Raymond — and I think Nick's a fool to trust you.'

She got up, moved for the door. Raymond called after her:

'How are Nick and O'Connor hitting it off?'

She smiled, showing her teeth.

'Nick sees things my way about O'Connor — and you can tell Miss Peters to leave Nick alone. I'll do something about that dame if she tries to cut me out.'

Elsa went through the door and slammed it behind her. Raymond grinned and offered Kirk a cigarette. Kirk refused, rolled one of his own. They lit up.

'Well,' Raymond said, 'what's new in town? I like to keep up with things. I guess you and Nick have got it all figured, huh?'

He inhaled cigarette smoke, blew it out in a sighing stream. Kirk didn't seem inclined to talk; he got up from his desk and came round to face Raymond. Close-up, his hare-lip gave him a nasty expression. His stoop, and shifty eyes made Raymond wary.

'I'll get on fine without your help,' Kirk said deliberately. 'You'd do as well to get out of town. I'm running the police department now.'

Raymond smiled.

'Archer told me to get out of town too. Look what happened to him.'

'Me and Nick's got things the way we want them. Bear that in mind, Raymond. Keep your nose clean — and now, get out. I'm a busy man.'

'Sure.' Raymond nodded casually. 'There's O'Connor — and Underhill. They bothering you?'

Kirk laughed. He didn't need to say anything; Raymond got the idea there would only be one mob in Lynx Falls pretty soon. He went along the passage, noting Traill's men hanging around. He drew a cop aside, asked:

'What's the idea of Nick's boys inhabiting City Hall?'

The cop looked surprised.

'Haven't you heard? The acting chief is swearing them in as specials. We're going to have a mighty powerful police force in town from now on.'

Raymond went down the steps of City Hall to the street with a grim expression on his face. It looked as if Traill meant business. Getting his mob sworn in as police was smart thinking on Nick's part; it would give him a legal out on any shooting he wanted done. Lynx Falls was in for another blood bath.

He moved along to Grant Street, turned left, passed a rusty iron fence and the laundry, to reach O'Connor's pool room. There didn't seem to be anybody about apart from the barman.

Raymond called for whisky, and said:
'Where's the boss?'
'What's it to you?' the barman returned carelessly.
'I've got news for him.'
'Yeah?'

Raymond poured the whisky down his throat, enjoying its warmth.

'Yeah,' he said flatly. 'O'Connor will want this news in a hurry. It concerns Nick's latest move. See what I mean?'

The barman nodded.

'You'll find him down the road. A

warehouse on a deserted lot. He's holed up there with his mob until he figures the score. Nick's got him worried.'

Raymond went outside and walked Grant till he neared the outskirts of the town. The warehouse stood alone on a barren strip of ground; there was no cover within fifty yards for anyone approaching it. O'Connor had picked a nice place to defend.

Raymond walked across the yard, towards the door. He didn't miss the gun covering his every movement. A voice shouted:

'What d'you want?'

Raymond kept still, his hands on view. He called back:

'I've some news for O'Connor. He'll want to hear what I've got for him.'

There was a pause. Raymond guessed his speech was being relayed to the bootlegger. The voice came again:

'Okay. Come on in — and keep your hands where I can see them.'

A door opened and Raymond walked through. The guard had a shot-gun and he looked as if he knew how to use it.

Another gangster took charge of Raymond and led him down cellar steps. The whole place reeked of the smell of whisky; the stuff was everywhere; in bottles, stacked in cases; in drums lining the walls; leaking across the floor from a still.

O'Connor had overlooked one point in choosing his warehouse as a hideout. The whisky would burn like petrol if Traill got near enough to fire it. The place was a death-trap.

In the cellar, O'Connor's mob were drinking and cleaning guns. There were fifteen men left in the bootlegger's outfit — enough to cause Traill a lot of trouble if O'Connor made a fight of it. Through a door, O'Connor and Hawkeye were sitting on the only two chairs in the warehouse. Neither of them got up.

The large man was still wearing the check shirt under slacks and sweater; Raymond wondered if he bothered to change his underclothes. His tough face was wet with sweat and he kneaded his hands constantly, cracking the knuckle-joints.

'What is it, Raymond? And it had

better be straight.'

Hawkeye had a .38 revolver in his left hand. His other arm was still in a sling. Sitting down, he looked even more like a little boy, despite the exaggerated drape and padded shoulders of his suit. His one good eye glared at Raymond.

'You bet it had better be straight,' he grunted.

Raymond smiled and leaned against the wall. He picked up a whisky bottle, pulled the bung and lifted the neck to his lips. He drank deeply, replaced the cork and set down the bottle. He wiped his mouth, said:

'Good stuff, O'Connor. Remind me to buy a bottle sometime.'

Hawkeye moved the revolver threateningly.

'What's Nick up to?' he demanded.

Raymond ignored the gunman, spoke directly at O'Connor:

'Kirk is swearing in Traill's mob as specials. You can figure out what that means without me telling you.'

The large man swore bitterly.

Raymond said: 'He's out to get you,

O'Connor. Nick aims to run Lynx Falls himself. Your only chance is to team up with Underhill and Fawkes — Nick's after them too. Between the three of you, it might be possible to bump Nick and take over. But I wouldn't bet on your chances if you run alone — remember, Nick has the rest of Archer's men on his side now that Kirk is taking his orders. That gives him the strongest mob in Lynx Falls.'

'The rat,' O'Connor said. 'Turning on me, after I got him out of jail. It's the blonde's fault — that bitch set him against me.'

'Yeah, Elsa,' Hawkeye said, fingering his gun lovingly. 'I'll put hot lead in her when I see her again!'

Raymond looked round at the whisky barrels.

'You want to get out of here before Nick finds you,' he drawled.

'You kidding? This is a good place to fight it out.'

Raymond said: 'Remember the road-house? Whisky burns too.'

He left a worried gangster as he went

back to the street. O'Connor was on edge. He'd start throwing lead the minute he caught sight of one of Traill's mob — and that would lead to another showdown. Raymond was pleased with the way things were going.

He dropped in at a drug-store and pushed a nickel in the 'phone box. He wanted to get Dr. Fawkes in on this.

He said: 'Fawkes? This is Raymond. I thought you might like to know that Kirk is swearing in Traill's gang as specials. I guess he's after you.'

Fawkes laughed in his jovial way. His voice boomed through the receiver:

'You're crazy. I'm not in Nick's way.'

'No? You've been seeing a lot of Elsa — and Nick doesn't like that.'

'Elsa? That's strictly business. I wouldn't cut in with Nick's dame, he knows that.'

But a little doubt had crept into Fawkes's voice. He didn't boom quite so loudly. The blackmailer was getting scared.

'Does he?' Raymond said. 'Then you won't mind telling him so when he calls with Verd and the boys. On the other hand, O'Connor is interested in teaming up with you — if you feel like it. You might mention the idea to Underhill when you see him — he's another on the list for a wooden box.'

Raymond replaced the telephone and left the drug store. He walked up Grant Street, to Main, whistling. He thought Nick Traill might get a little more opposition than he bargained for — and some more of the Lynx Falls gangs would die before long.

He decided to head for Northwood and report progress to Dot. If Jerry made himself scarce for a while, he might get the chance to show how much he loved her. Momentarily, he cursed himself for sending the editor out to Northwood; it cramped his style to have Jerry around when he was longing to take Dot in his arms and kiss her.

He returned to the Palace hotel for his car and headed north for the Peters' residence.

9

It was evening when Raymond drove back from Northwood. Shadows and moonlight made a mosaic pattern on the road leading into town. The air was still and the trees looked like silent sentinels.

He rode down Main Street, noting the lack of people on the sidewalks; only Kirk's men were about. Lynx Falls was like a ghost town, with the inhabitants waiting for terror to strike again. There was an atmosphere of tension blanketing the dimly lit streets.

Raymond parked his Cadillac and entered the foyer of the Palace hotel. Across the street, the *Gazette* office showed a yellow light; the noise of printing presses clattered from the building at the rear. Two uniformed cops with dirty buttons idled past, their eyes searching out the shadows.

Bill Raymond went into the bar and called for whisky. He leaned on the

136

counter, smoking a cigarette. The place was empty, except for the bartender who was mopping unenthusiastically at yesterday's beer stains.

'Anything new in town?' Raymond asked.

The barman shrugged.

'Nothing exciting — yet.'

Raymond puffed at his cigarette. There was something in the way the barman spoke that made him ask:

'But you're expecting — what?'

'You saw the *Gazette* editorial?' Raymond nodded. The barman went on: 'Kirk's men have been hanging around the office over the road, all day. I guess Goodrich will be buzzard-meat as soon as he shows up.'

'That so?' Raymond said.

He thought Kirk would go on waiting a long time before Jerry went near the office again. The editor was safely hidden at Dot's place — and Raymond had told him to stay there.

He crossed to the window and looked out. The two cops were still patrolling up and down outside the office. Further

137

along the street, a police wagon without lights had pulled into the curb. Raymond's lips tightened perceptibly; Traill had given the word to get Jerry Goodrich.

He went up to 107 and stretched out on the bed, smoking and thinking. Outside, night clouds gathered and darkness descended over Main Street. Raymond wondered who would strike first, Traill or O'Connor. And Underhill was strangely silent — the lawyer would be waiting to see which way the wind blew. Underhill had brains; he wouldn't go against the gambler until he was sure of his ground.

Raymond stubbed out his cigarette. That left Fawkes — and Elsa. Maybe he could do something to precipitate the coming gang war if —

An explosion rocked the Palace hotel. Windows shattered with a tinkling of glass; the curtains billowed inwards and the sky was red with flame. Raymond came off the bed in a hurry; he stared down into the street. The *Gazette* office was on fire — Kirk had got tired of waiting and had thrown a bomb through the window. Jerry Goodrich wouldn't be using his office again until it was rebuilt.

He could see Kirk down below, snapping orders at his men. Cops moved to the printing shop at the rear; shortly afterwards, the sound of the presses stopped. The *Gazette* had closed down — until Nick Traill found someone to run the paper his way.

Raymond smiled grimly; Jerry would thank him for keeping him out of the way now. If the editor had been in his office, he'd be dead at this minute. Raymond went down to the call box to 'phone Jerry and tell him what happened. He never reached the booth.

Kirk came through the foyer with half-a-dozen men at his back. A hand-rolled cigarette dangled under his hare-lip.

'Raymond, I want you down at City Hall. You coming quiet?'

Bill Raymond didn't like the way he said it.

'What's biting you?' he drawled.

'We don't like guys who throw bombs around,' Kirk said. 'You were seen to blow up the *Gazette* office. I've got witnesses.'

Raymond turned sideways to present a smaller target. A Luger came out from his pocket and pointed at the acting chief.

'Your witnesses are liars!'

The Luger stopped Kirk cold. One of his men went for a gun; Raymond shot it out of his hand. Kirk said:

'That finishes you, Raymond. Resisting arrest and shooting a cop — I'm going to take you in.'

Raymond jeered: 'Are those Nick's orders?'

Kirk flushed. His hare-lip quivered.

'Get him!'

Raymond snapped a shot into the grouped men and ran for the rear door. A slug buried itself in the woodwork as he went through. He stopped to jam a chair against the door, to hold up pursuit, then darted along a passage, out into the yard behind the hotel.

Heavy feet pounded after him as he raced for his car. The Cadillac started easily. Kirk came round the corner and a cop fired twice as the car jerked into forward motion and nosed out on to Main Street. Kirk shouted something and a police wagon gave chase.

Raymond stamped his foot on the accelerator and headed south. He intended hiding out in Northwood, but first he had to shake off the cops on his tail. He remembered O'Connor's mob at the warehouse — maybe he could give them something to shoot at.

He roared across Central Plaza with the traffic signals at red. A cop tried to stop him; Raymond kept going. The cop got out of the way. The wagon behind wasn't as fast, but the men inside were firing all the time. Slugs chewed into the back of the Cadillac.

Raymond passed City Hall and Elsa's house, gaining a slight lead. At Grant, he swung left, tyres screeching in protest as he rounded the corner on two wheels with the accelerator hard down. By the time the police wagon turned the bend, he was out of range.

The laundry and O'Connor's pool room flashed by. He reached the outskirts of the town and the deserted lot where the warehouse stood. Raymond swung the car off the road. It bounced over the curb and headed across the waste ground, skirting the warehouse. The police wagon followed, siren screaming, guns blazing.

O'Connor must have figured the score. Raymond stopped sweating when no slugs came his way from the darkened warehouse. The bootlegger's mob waited till the police wagon was twenty yards off, then they opened up with tommy-guns. Maybe they thought the cops were after them.

A hail of lead poured out from the warehouse. It caught the police wagon dead-centre and riddled it to pieces. The wagon, driverless, crashed into a wall. The petrol tank exploded. No-one came out alive.

Raymond didn't stop. He swung left again, along Sherman to Columbus Avenue. He stopped at a drug store to make a 'phone call. He had to inform Dot and Jerry about the new set-up; warn them he was wanted by the police, that Nick had given the word to get him. Things were moving towards the climax and they had to be prepared for trouble.

He pushed a nickel in the slot and dialled. The ringing sound went on and on; nobody answered. Raymond called the exchange.

'I can't get an answer from Northwood 22793. Can you help me?'

The operator went to work. She reported back:

'I'm sorry sir, there seems to be no one at home. Our connection is perfect.'

Cold sweat started out on Raymond's brow. Both Dot and Jerry should have been at the Northwood house. He ran for his Cadillac and drove like a madman. Something was wrong; there was no reason why they shouldn't have answered the telephone.

It was after eleven and the road out of town deserted. Raymond urged every ounce of speed he could get out of his car. The moonlight was bright, the air still. In the distance, the hills merged with the darkness.

His car lights cut a brilliant swathe through the gloom. Bill Raymond was worried. His face was taut, his hands rigid. The Luger in his pocket was heavy. He was thinking of Dot — and Nick Traill. He'd tried not to think of what might have happened to the girl he loved . . .

But if Traill had harmed her, Raymond was going after the gambler, and his gun wouldn't be silent until he had exacted full revenge.

★   ★   ★

Jerry Goodrich nestled behind the curve of his brier. He puffed contentedly and watched Dot in the armchair across the fire in the library of her Northwood home. Her face was a constantly changing mask of emotions. He read there, love and fear, anxiety and longing. He said:

'Why don't you go to bed, Dot? You need some sleep — and you won't help Bill by worrying yourself sick. He's able to take care of himself.'

'I can't help worrying, Jerry. I wish I'd never asked him to take this job.'

Her dark eyes misted and she rubbed the freckle on her nose.

Jerry said: 'You know you don't mean that.'

He stretched his legs and tapped down the tobacco in his pipe. The clock on the wall crept round towards ten o'clock.

Dorothy Peters rose, yawning.

'I guess you're right. I'll go upstairs. You going to sit up?'

'Yeah. Bill may 'phone some more news.'

'You'll let me know?'

He grinned: 'Sure!'

She said goodnight and left Jerry to the library fire. He leafed through a magazine, hardly seeing the words. He put it down, paced the room restlessly. It was hell, loving Dot, and knowing that she cared only for Bill Raymond. Bill was a good sort — but why did he have to cut in with Dot?

He sat down again. He dropped the magazine and stared into the fire; his pipe went out. It was warm in the library and, presently, he dozed off.

He woke suddenly, at the sound of a car driving up to the house. He sat up, his brain clearing; Bill must have important news to come back at this hour. He started for the door, then stopped; the butler would let Raymond in.

Car doors slammed — but no sound came at the front door. Jerry frowned. Suppose . . . he stopped guessing as the French windows opened violently and Nick Traill came into the room. Behind him, Verd carried a blue-nosed automatic. Traill had two more men with him.

Goodrich shouted: 'Dot! Look out — it's . . . '

Verd's automatic crashed loudly. There was a puff of smoke, a long, stabbing flame — and hot lead tore into the editor's stomach. He went over backwards, holding his middle, and moaning. His head hit a chair, knocking off his glasses.

Verd's thin lips curled in a sneer, his blue eyes flashed coldly. The cleft-chinned gunman crossed the room and kicked Goodrich in the mouth.

'Stop whining, you puppy!'

The butler came in, alarmed at the shot. Verd spun round, fired again. The bullet smashed into the butler's chest, into his heart, killing him instantly. He died without a sound.

Nick Traill laughed. His swarthy face gleamed in the fire-light and the scar running down his cheek twitched.

'Get the girl,' he said.

The two men went through to the hall. Dot was coming down the stairs; she'd heard the shooting and wanted to find out what it was all about. Traill's men grabbed her and dragged her into the library. She saw Jerry on the floor, moving a little and moaning; blood seeped through his hands folded over his stomach.

She cried out: 'Jerry!' and tried to go to him.

The men held her tight so she had to stand and watch Jerry in his agony. Nick Traill went up to her, his eyes alight with vicious glee. He kissed her, and said:

'You're coming with me, Miss Peters. I told you I'd marry you — and, by God, I'm going to!'

She tried to scratch his face with her nails. One of the men hit her. Traill laughed.

'I like a girl with spirit. Tie her hands and gag her — then take her out to the car. I'll deal with her myself.'

Jerry tried to get up. His face was a mask of pain, and the strength was leaving his body, but he had to save Dot. He crawled forward . . .

Dot, bound and gagged, was hustled to the waiting car. Verd went with them. Nick stared down at the editor, smiling viciously.

'I'm leaving you to die, Goodrich,' he snarled. 'A man takes a long time with a slug in his stomach — and it's damn painful. You can think of me with Miss Peters while you're lying there. Wish us a swell honeymoon!'

Jerry tried to grab Traill's ankles. Nick stamped on his fingers, turned away to the door. Jerry cursed him, moaning, coughing blood.

Verd was at the wheel of the green coupé. Traill got in beside him. In the back, Dot was firmly held between the two hoodlums.

'Get going,' Nick snapped.

The coupé moved off, lights doused.

Nick turned to face Dot. He said:

'Tomorrow, we're going to be married. Then you'll make over all your money to me. After the honeymoon, maybe I'll let you go, or perhaps you'd rather join the gang?'

Dot shuddered. She was thinking about Jerry, dying with a bullet in his stomach — and Bill . . . where was Bill? He'd save her.

The coupé travelled fast, cutting across country to the south-west. She began to wonder where Traill was taking her, and watched the road. Bright moonlight enabled her to trace their route. She recognised Delaware Park as the car entered the drive of Underhills yellow brick house. They took her inside.

The house was full of Traill's men and, in a front downstairs room, Underhill was tied in a chair. The lawyer's sour face was a mask of blood where he'd been beaten up; his pince-nez were smashed. Nick gloated:

'I've got her, Underhill; now she can sign the papers you've drawn up — then it'll all be legal. That's how I like to get my money, the legal way.' He grinned. 'I'm a guy that just hates to use force!'

Elsa was sitting on a settee. The blonde looked from Nick to the girl, and snapped:

'Remember what you said, Nick — it's only her money you're interested in. I won't stand for any monkey business.'

Traill laughed.

'Sure,' he grinned, 'only her money — why else would she interest a guy like me?'

Verd stared at the ceiling and whistled a few bars of *What is it my baby has that makes me happy?*

Traill said: 'The wedding is fixed for tomorrow afternoon. As soon as I've got my wife's signature on the document transferring her fortune to me, our marriage comes to an end. A rather fatal end for Mrs. Traill.'

'That's okay,' Elsa said. 'I wouldn't mind slitting her throat myself. And I'm staying here to-night, Nick.'

'That isn't necessary, Elsa,' Nick protested.

The blonde's smile was cold. She knew

she was losing her looks; she'd had a hard life and had to use a lot of powder to hide the lines appearing on her face. And Nick saw her too often without her war-paint . . . he was beginning to lose interest. Dot Peters was young and lovely — and Elsa didn't intend to be replaced.

'I'm staying,' she said flatly.

'Okay, Elsa. Miss Peters doesn't mean a thing to me.'

But already he was thinking of a way to get rid of the blonde.

Dot was marched upstairs and locked in — alone. Though she hated Elsa, she was glad the blonde was in the house; she didn't think Nick would bother her with Elsa around.

But what about tomorrow? With horror, she realized that the gambler meant to go through with the marriage — and Elsa wouldn't be able to stop him. Tears welled up in her eyes. She loved Bill — and tomorrow . . .

Dot dried her eyes. She forced herself to keep calm. Bill Raymond would find her gone, Jerry — she had to face the word — *dead*, and he'd guess what had happened. He'd come after her. Yes, Bill would save her — she had only to keep Nick at arms length until he arrived.

A terrifying thought overcame her. Did Bill know that Traill was at Underhill's house? Suppose he didn't find out till too late — till *after* she was married.

10

The house was silent, but lights still showed in the library. Bill Raymond drove his Cadillac to the front door of the Peters' house, left the engine running as he went up the steps, gun in hand. The door was open and the stone lions ignored him.

He almost fell over the dead body of the butler as he went through the door, into the library. There was a lot of blood on the carpet. Jerry Goodrich lay in a heap, his arm outstretched for the telephone he couldn't quite reach. Raymond turned him over.

Jerry's eyes opened as Raymond moved him. He whispered:

'Nick . . . Traill — got . . . Dot — '

Raymond cursed. Quickly he examined the editor's wound; he'd been shot once, through the stomach, and had lost a lot of blood. There wasn't much Raymond could do for him. He used the 'phone to call the hospital and get an ambulance sent out. If Jerry received medical aid right away, he might live.

But Dot! Raymond was baffled; where had Nick taken her? He realized that he had no idea where the gambler was hiding out. Who would know? Elsa — or Kirk. Kirk was looking for him — okay, if the acting chief wanted trouble, he'd give it to him!

Bill Raymond left the house in a hurry. His Cadillac burned the road back to town. He pulled up outside Elsa's house and hammered on the door. The girl who opened it had sultry eyes and pouting lips. She slurred:

'In a hurry big boy? Can't wait for — '

Raymond was in no mood for playing games. He gripped the girl's arm till she yelped with pain.

'Where's Elsa?'

'Let go, you brute! She's — oh, you're hurting! — with Nick.'

'Where?'

The girl writhed under his savage grip.

'I don't know. If I knew I'd tell you — but I don't!'

Raymond flung her from him. The girl was telling the truth, and he was wasting time. He went back to the street. Kirk came out of City Hall with two cops. Raymond jumped into the Cadillac and drove after them. He loosed off a couple of shots, scattering the cops; braked to a halt and shoved the Luger under Kirk's nose.

'Get in!' he snapped.

Kirk's face went deathly pale as he saw the burning fury in Raymond's eyes. He got in; and Raymond shoved the car into top gear. It leapt forward, racing out of Lynx Falls.

Kirk mumbled: 'Take it easy, Raymond. I didn't mean any harm.'

Raymond ignored him. Kirk was scared to fight it out in the car; they were travelling too fast to take risks. Raymond pulled up with a jerk when they reached open country. Kirk's head plunged forward, hitting the dashboard and half-stunning him. Raymond took his gun away and pushed him out of the car.

Kirk backed away. He was scared. Raymond's face was a mask of bitter rage;

his panther-like body was tensed for the kill. Kirk knew what was coming to him and he shivered with fear.

'Where's Traill?' Raymond demanded.

Kirk shook his head. His voice quavered:

'I don't know. Honest to God, I don't know.'

Raymond brought up his knee, slammed it into Kirk's groin. The acting chief groaned, bent forward. Raymond hit him in the face with his Luger, spoiling his hare-lip.

Kirk said, again: 'I don't know — I'd tell — '

Raymond hit him again; and went on hitting him till his face was a mask of blood. Kirk slumped to the ground. Raymond kicked him again and again, saying:

'Where's Traill? Where's Traill?'

He was panting with fury, thinking of Dot and scared of what might happen to her. He hadn't thought it possible to care so much for one person — but then, he'd never been in love before.

Kirk moaned: 'For God's sake, Raymond, I tell you I've no idea where Nick is hiding out.'

At last, Raymond gave up. It was obvious that Kirk was speaking the truth; he'd never have taken so much punishment if he could have escaped by ratting on the gambler. Raymond walked back to his car, leaving Kirk on the ground. The acting chief blubbered through a froth of blood; it was going to be some time before he felt like walking back to Lynx Falls.

Raymond drove furiously towards town. He stopped at the first call box he came to and rang Dr. Fawkes. The blackmailer sounded sleepy:

'Who's calling?'

'Raymond. Do you know where Nick Traill is — I want to find him in a hurry.'

Fawkes didn't know. Raymond rang off and dialled Underhill. The 'phone rang a long time and the lawyer's voice sounded strange when he answered.

'Nick Traill,' Raymond snapped. 'Where can I find him?'

'Haven't seen him,' Underhill said in a strained voice. 'I'm afraid I can't help you.'

Bill Raymond replaced the 'phone and

157

went back to his car. He had no way of knowing that Underhill spoke with a gun at his head and Traill laughing softly in the background. He racked his brain for a clue to the gambler's hiding place — and failed to find anything that would give him a lead.

In desperation, he headed for O'Connor's warehouse. The bootlegger laughed over the way Raymond had led the cops to their death. He seemed very happy about it.

Raymond said: 'Nick's kidnapped Dorothy Peters. You wouldn't know where he might take her?'

Hawkeye said: 'We should worry over a dame.'

'Yeah,' O'Connor grunted, looking hard at Raymond. 'What's the Peters' girl to you?'

Raymond knew he was on dangerous ground; he daren't let these men know he was working for Dot, cleaning up the town on her instructions. He didn't want them to think he was personally interested, either. He replied:

'Use your head, O'Connor. Miss Peters

owns most of Lynx Falls on paper. Traill will force her into marrying him, to get control of her fortune. That way, no-one can move against him.'

O'Connor was impressed by Raymond's analysis of the situation. Hawkeye still seemed suspicious. Raymond went on:

'Nick will have his hands full with the girl, arranging the marriage, forcing her to sign papers. If we strike now, we can catch him off-guard. But I don't know where to find him.'

Hawkeye grinned.

'Nick always fancied the Peters' dame. I guess you're right — he'll be busy with her. We ought to go gunning for him now, boss.'

'Yeah,' O'Connor said, cracking his knuckle joints and thinking about it. 'Kirk or Elsa would know.'

Raymond said, grimly: 'Elsa's with Nick. I worked on Kirk a little — he doesn't know.'

O'Connor scratched his head.

'I dunno where he'd be,' he admitted. He thought about it some more, then turned to Hawkeye. 'Take a couple of the boys and see if you can get a lead on Nick. I like Raymond's idea. We'll go after Traill as soon as we know where to find him.'

'Okay, boss.'

Hawkeye went off, a small boy with exaggerated shoulders and a .38 in his hand. His right arm was still in a sling and he looked at Raymond as if he'd like to do something about that.

Raymond fretted impatiently. He chain-smoked, thinking of Dot in Traill's power. He didn't like it. But there was nothing he could do till he located the gambler. He paced the cellar restlessly.

After an hour, he couldn't stand it any more. He said:

'I'm going out to look for Nick. I'll let you know if I find anything.'

O'Connor said: 'Sure. We'll know what to do then.'

Raymond went out to his Cadillac and drove into the centre of Lynx Falls. There weren't many people about, but he stopped everyone he saw and asked them for news of Traill. He drew a blank.

A couple of cops spotted him. They knew Kirk wanted him and gave chase. Raymond got away, but he realized how difficult it was going to be for him to operate in the open. In desperation, he returned to the warehouse. Hawkeye was back — and he hadn't learnt anything.

★ ★ ★

Dorothy Peters felt as if she were living a nightmare. The night hours had passed in an agony of sleeplessness; Traill hadn't bothered her, but she knew that was only because Elsa was in the house. She couldn't face the breakfast a surly-mouthed mobster brought her; she longed to see Bill's rugged face again, to slip into the safety of his arms.

The morning passed. The sun moved steadily across the sky, marking off the hours to her forced marriage. Her spirits sank; she'd never felt so depressed, so terrified before. She went round her prison again, hopelessly looking for some way to escape.

There were bars across the window,

and the glass wouldn't break; she'd tried that. The door was locked. She sat down on the bed. If only Bill would find her in time . . .

A key turned in the lock. The door opened and Nick Traill came in. His swarthy face gleamed as he looked at her. He took her in his arms, forced kisses on her trembling lips.

'In two hours,' he said, 'we'll be married. Everything's fixed.' He laughed as she struggled, broke away from him. 'I like a girl who puts up a fight,' he told her. 'I'm going to enjoy being married to you.'

'You swine,' Dot sobbed. 'Bill will kill you — '

'Raymond doesn't know you're here,' Traill sneered. 'Maybe I'll let him know — afterwards. He'll come a-running — right into a trap!'

Dot bit her lips to stop the tears that threatened to engulf her. The idea of being used as bait to trap the man she loved horrified her; she hated Nick Traill as she'd never before hated any man. She tried to get at him, to hurt him.

Traill held her off easily. He flung her from him.

'You'd better make up your mind to be nice to me,' he said. 'But first, there are some papers to sign. Then I'll get rid of Elsa — that blonde's been hanging around too long. I'm tired of her.'

The door closed behind him and Dot was alone once more. She shivered with fear. She'd never submit to Traill — never! She'd kill herself first . . .

The sun moved slowly across the sky. An hour passed. She looked at herself in the mirror; her dark hair was all over the place; her lipstick was smeared; She automatically straightened her hair; she wouldn't want Bill to see her looking a wreck . . . if he ever came.

She stood by the window, watching the road, praying for a sight of his Cadillac. But it never came. She imagined him searching for her, frustrated and angry; she didn't know the police were looking for him, that he was forced to remain under cover. Her nightmare dragged on and courage ebbed away.

One of Traill's men brought her lunch

on a tray; she left it untouched. She was alone with her thoughts, frightened and restless. Suppose Bill did come? Traill's men outnumbered him twenty to one; he'd be killed before her very eyes. She paced the room, hoping and praying.

Footsteps sounded on the stairs. The door opened and two mobsters entered.

One laughed: 'Feeling fine for your wedding, beautiful?'

The other man said nothing; he tied her hands in front of her. They marched her downstairs between them. Nick Traill was waiting with a preacher, a gaunt man with a starched white collar and a smirk on his face.

'Ah, the happy bride!' he said jovially.

Dot tried to keep her voice level, but it trailed off despite her effort.

'I'm being forced into this marriage. I don't want to marry this man. I hate him!'

The preacher smiled and ignored her. Nick said:

'You're wasting your time, Miss Peters. The preacher is paid to do what *I* tell him.'

'It won't be legal. I'll — '

'Any marriage performed by me,' the preacher assured her, 'is completely legal. Now, can we start?'

Traill had a ring which he handed to the preacher. The man chanted the service without enthusiasm or interest.

'Do you take this woman for your lawfully wedded wife?'

Traill said: 'I do.'

Dot tried to break away. Two thugs held her still. She was forced to listen to the farce.

'Do you take this man for your lawfully wedded husband?'

'She does!' Traill said.

'No! No!' Dot screamed hysterically. 'Stop it — stop this blasphemy!'

The preacher ignored her, babbled on. He forced the ring onto her finger; Dot couldn't stop him with her hands tied and two men holding her.

'I pronounce you man and wife,' the preacher said.

Nick laughed.

'How about a kiss, *Mrs. Traill*?'

Dot bit his lip as he bent over her. Nick

struck her viciously.

'I'll teach you better manners before I've finished with you. Now you'll sign some papers, giving me complete control over your interests in this town.'

Dot's face turned pale. All through the ceremony, she'd been hoping Bill would turn up. Now it was too late. Her heart sank and tears rolled down her cheeks.

Verd lifted a whisky glass and toasted, ironically:

'To the happy pair!'

He tossed the whisky down his throat and laughed.

11

The wind from the west was rising again as Bill Raymond drove towards the river. It was lunch-time, but Raymond was in no mood for eating. His bronzed face wore a stubble and the rings under his eyes indicated that he hadn't slept that night. His eyes held a cold, pitiless light and his mouth was a taut line. He had one desire driving him on; find Nick Traill and kill him!

O'Connor's men had been unable to trace the gambler; nor had Raymond, though he had searched Lynx Falls till he was sick of the place. The only good news he'd had was that Jerry Goodrich was out of danger; the editor would be in hospital a while yet, but he would recover.

Now, Raymond was on his way to visit Dr. Fawkes. He hoped the blackmailer, through Elsa, might have learnt something by this time. If not, he intended to call on Underhill. The Cadillac skirted the suburbs of Lynx Falls, following the road that led from O'Connor's warehouse to the river.

Raymond tried to keep his mind off Dorothy Peters. He knew he could do no good by torturing himself with visions of her. But the mental images kept coming back to torment him. Raymond concentrated his thoughts on Nick Traill — he'd find the gambler and kill him with his own hands!

Dr. Fawkes' house nestled in the foothills; a cream and chromium eyesore amid lovely country. Raymond parked his car and went in by a French window, not bothering the Japanese house-boy. The low muttering of voices attracted him to a door off the main passage. He opened the door and stepped into a large room that was half in darkness.

A semi-circle of chairs held a dozen or more middle-aged and expensively dressed women; there was one man who looked as if he were on the verge of a nervous breakdown, and a youth of eighteen with a bow tie and an air of condescension. The room was draped with black velvet and heavy curtains blocked out the sunlight. Spluttering candles gave a faint yellow light and an exotic perfume.

Fawkes was sprawled in a chair at the hub from which the semi-circle of chairs radiated. His eyes were closed and his voice came out in a high-pitched squeak. Raymond guessed he had gate-crashed one of the blackmailer's seances.

The squeaky voice complained:

'I feel a disturbing influence in the room . . .'

Raymond grated: 'Like hell you do! I'm looking for Nick Traill. Elsa will do — '

Fawkes' body shuddered; he writhed as if in a trance. A woman grabbed Raymond's arm and dragged him to an empty chair.

She shushed angrily: 'Be quiet, young man! It's dangerous to distract a medium when he's in trance. Your mundane business will have to wait.'

The others in the group glared at Raymond. Fawkes' voice came again, high-pitched and squeaky as he simulated his spirit-guide:

'I have a message for someone in the room. A man.'

Raymond tensed. Something told him that Fawkes was taking this method of telling him what he wanted to know. He loathed the idea of sitting still and pandering to Fawkes' trickery, but he had to hear what the man said.

The voice went on: 'The message comes from a girl with fair hair . . . ' Elsa, Raymond guessed. ' . . . she wants him to know that the person he seeks has taken refuge with a man of law. Her thoughts are most violent — I feel I cannot go on . . . '

Raymond came out of his seat, ignoring the woman who tried to hold him down. Underhill! Fawkes had told him that Nick Traill was at the lawyer's house. Elsa must have had a row with Nick — obviously over Dot. The blonde wanted him to kill Nick; that was the reference to 'violent thoughts.'

He smiled; Elsa was going to get her wish. Raymond went through the door to the passage. In the hall, he found a telephone. He used it.

'O'Connor's pool room.' Raymond recognised the voice of the barman. He said:

'This is Raymond. Go to the warehouse and tell O'Connor he'll find Traill at Underhill's Delaware Park home.'

He rang off, hurried out to his car. He drove fast, taking the road round the lake, passing the falls. The west wind swept water spray over him; the wind was rising for another gale. It was the west wind that brought bloodshed to Lynx Falls.

Leaving the river, Raymond picked up Juniper Drive and headed north. He reached Delaware Park, braked to a halt as he came into view of Underhill's yellow brick house. He did the rest on foot; he wanted to take Traill by surprise.

Raymond was glad the lawyer didn't have a large garden; he was able to take advantage of the shoulder-high edge to get close to the house without being seen. He followed the wall to a window and looked through.

Underhill was tied in a chair, his body limp, head down on his chest. He had been shot through the right eye and blood stained his face where it had poured from the empty socket. The lawyer wasn't going to interfere in Lynx Falls business again.

Raymond went round the house, looking for a way in. Traill's mob seemed to have made it their headquarters. There were men in every room, talking, smoking, drinking, cleaning guns. One window was half-open and voices drifted out. Raymond heard laughter.

'Nick's upstairs with the missus — can you imagine him *marrying* a dame!'

Raymond trembled with anger; he had to exert tremendous self-control to stop himself emptying his Luger into the room. Desperately, he looked for a way in; he had to rescue Dot somehow. Upstairs ... his eyes fixed on the ivy covering the walls of the house. Would the creeper bear his weight?

He went round the side of the house, where the ivy was thickest. No one saw him. He reached upwards, grabbed two handfuls of creeper and swung his feet off the ground. The ivy sagged, but held him. He dug both feet into the tangled vines and reached upwards again. Hand over hand, he climbed the wall to a window.

He smashed the glass with his gun and swung himself through. A passage ran the length of the upper storey, and rooms branched off it. If any of the gangsters downstairs heard the sound of glass breaking, they took no notice. Raymond went along the passage, opening doors, looking for Dot.

He heard her voice coming from behind a door at the far end of the passage and ran forward. He pushed open the door and went in.

Dot was on one side of the bed, Traill on the other. She held a broken piece of china jug and was defending herself with the sharp edge. Traill had a jagged gash on one wrist and he was swearing.

Raymond snapped: 'Move over Dot — I'll take care of Nick.'

She turned, incredulous at the sound of his voice. Her face lit up.

'Bill! Thank God you got here in time.'

Traill recovered from his amazement. Snarling, he went for his gun. Raymond couldn't shoot because Dot was between

173

him and the gambler. Traill's shot went wide; he sprang for the door, shouting:

'Verd — Raymond's here. Get him!'

Raymond pushed Dot aside to get at Traill. The gambler swung his arm, knocking the girl into Raymond. They crashed to the floor. Raymond rolled sideways, clipping a shot at Traill as he went through the door. His slug tore the fabric of Traill's coat, but didn't stop him.

Feet sounded on the stairs. The gang was coming up to deal with Raymond. Bullets sped into the room.

'Keep down!' Raymond shouted at Dot.

He wriggled towards the door, firing at shadow movements in the passage. Traill called:

'You're trapped, Raymond. You might as well give yourself up.'

Raymond fired in the direction of his voice. Traill laughed. His men shot back. Raymond swung the door shut; desperately, he moved the heavy wardrobe across the door. For the moment, they were safe. The mobsters outside couldn't open the door and their slugs buried themselves harmlessly in the thick walls of the wardrobe.

The tension went out of Dot Peters. She flung herself into Raymond's arms, sobbing with relief, her body quivering with released emotion. Tears stained her cheeks as she kissed him.

'Bill; oh, Bill — I'm so glad you're here.'

Raymond held her tight, kissed her back. Then he pushed her off, said grimly:

'We're not out of it yet.'

His eyes flickered round the room, noting the steel bars across the window. Traill was right; they were trapped. The gangsters had brought up tommy-guns. They riddled the door with bullets; splinters of wood sprang across the room.

'Back against the wall,' Raymond snapped.

Dot obeyed, smiling happily. She knew everything would be all right now that Bill had come for her; she'd do anything he told her, without question. The wardrobe sagged and splintered under the barrage of machine-gun slugs; it wasn't going to last much longer. Already, cracks were showing.

Raymond reloaded his Luger. He fired through one of the cracks. He hit someone in the passage; the man groaned and one of the tommy-guns stopped. Raymond heard it hit the floor.

Verd's voice came: 'I'm going to get you, Raymond.'

They were battering at the door, slowly shifting the wardrobe, forcing open the door. Raymond kept firing steadily; he couldn't see any way out. All he could do was delay the end and pray that O'Connor would show up in time. He shoved the bed against the wardrobe. Bullets sprayed into the room.

Raymond caught a glimpse of a surly face over a machine-gun. He fired into the face. It dropped, blood spurting from one sightless eye. Traill's voice sneered.

'You can't last much longer, Raymond. Then I'll have the girl . . .'

Raymond swore violently. He emptied his gun at Traill's voice. The gambler laughed; he was keeping well back, leaving his men to do the fighting.

Raymond reloaded; he waited grimly. He didn't have many shells left, but he determined to make every one count — and to get Nick Traill before the end came.

The wardrobe went over with a crash. The bed was pushed back as the door opened. Raymond saw the snout of a gun poke into the room; he fired at the hand holding the gun.

Verd said: 'Now — get him!'

A mass of tough gangsters showed in the doorway. Raymond worked his trigger finger relentlessly, pumping slugs into the mob. Blood streaked his face where a bullet grazed him. He couldn't hold them any longer — this was it . . .

Downstairs, an explosion rocked the house. New gunfire started up. Traill's mob, disconcerted, gave way and retreated. It was Bill Raymond's turn to laugh.

'Start praying, Traill,' he shouted. 'O'Connor's looking for trouble!'

Nick Traill was running. Verd and his mob engaged the bootlegger's gang in pitched battle. Tommy-guns and grenades turned the quiet of Delaware Park to a hideous cacophony of sound. Raymond looked through the window; in the garden, O'Connor incited his men to wipe out Nick Traill.

It looked as if O'Connor was going to get things all his way. Hawkeye blazed away with his .38; the mob were driving Traill into a corner. There was no doubt that the bootlegger would have won the day if Kirk hadn't arrived with reinforcements.

Kirk came up with a wagon load of cops. O'Connor's men were caught between the cross-fire. Hawkeye went down, nearly chopped in half by machine-gun fire. The bootlegger tried to rally his men, but they'd had enough. They started to run for it.

O'Connor was out in the open, alone, deserted by his gang. He cursed virulently and stood his ground; he knew he wasn't going to come through alive — but he wasn't going to run before a dago. He stood there, an automatic in each hand, blasting sudden death to cops and crooks alike.

His end came violently. Someone threw a grenade in his face. O'Connor put up his arm to save himself. The bomb exploded, blowing off his arm and head. His bloody torso made a grotesque heap on the lawn.

Kirk and his cops were cleaning up. Solitary shots rang out as lone members of the bootlegger's outfit were caught and killed. Nick Traill had forgotten Raymond and the girl in the excitement.

Raymond gripped Dot's arm. He said: 'Let's get out of here.'

They hurried down the back stairs, out through the garden. Raymond's Cadillac was where he had left it; they got in and he drove away from the shambles. Dot nestled close to him, her head on his shoulder. She sighed happily — her expression changed, and she sat up.

She said, troubled: 'Bill, I forgot to tell you — I'm married to Nick Traill!'

Raymond laughed harshly.

'You'll be a widow soon!'

He was adding the score. Archer and Smitty, Underhill, O'Connor and Hawk-eye were dead. That left Dr. Fawkes and

Elsa — he had an idea Traill would be taking care of them as soon as the gambler got around to thinking who had betrayed him — and Traill, Verd and Kirk. Raymond didn't care who got the last two. But he wanted Nick Traill himself; he wanted to kill him for the way he'd tried to force himself on Dot.

As Raymond drove back to town the west wind blew across the hills, bending the trees before it. The wind was building up to gale force again, bringing new terror to Lynx Falls.

12

'She'll be all right here, Mr. Raymond.'

The old woman with greying hair who kept a florist's shop on Main Street smiled at Dot Peters. Raymond was pushing shells into his Luger. He said:

'I'm going after Nick Traill. Once he's out of the way, it'll be a cinch to clean up the small fry.'

Dot clung to him.

'Be careful, Bill. I couldn't stand it if anything happened to you.'

The florist took Dot's arm and made her sit down.

'Now, now, Miss Peters, you've had a bad time. Just you sit there and take it easy and I'll make some coffee. Mr. Raymond can look after himself; he's proved that all right.'

Raymond put the gun in his pocket. He bent over Dot and kissed her.

'I shan't be long,' he said grimly.

The old woman touched his arm.

'Don't worry about Miss Peters,' she smiled. 'I'll look after her now. She's safe enough here.'

Raymond nodded. He went through the door, out on to the street. Lynx Falls appeared deserted; the people were keeping off the streets till gang warfare stopped. Raymond got behind the wheel of his Cadillac and started the engine.

As he had anticipated, once he explained that he was a private detective engaged by Dot to run the crooks out of town, the florist had been all for them. Dot would be safe with the old woman while he tidied up a few loose ends. The florist hadn't forgotten how Raymond had saved her from Healey; she'd look after Dot.

Raymond drove down Main Street. He crossed Central Plaza as a police wagon came into town from the other direction. Kirk's men, badly depleted in numbers, were returning from the affair at Delaware Park. Kirk recognized Raymond's Cadillac; he remembered how the detective had beat him up — and he wanted revenge.

'Raymond!' he screamed at the driver. 'Get him!'

The police wagon swung across the road; its bumper hit the Cadillac's offside back mudguard, overturning it. Raymond came out, Luger in hand.

Kirk dropped from the wagon, a couple of cops at his back. His hare-lip was split where Raymond had hit him; he went for his gun, shouting:

'This is where you get yours, Raymond!'

Raymond fired into the cops behind the acting chief; they scattered. They'd had enough shooting for one day. That left Kirk alone, facing Raymond. He shot first.

Kirk's slug whined past Raymond's shoulder. The acting chief lost his nerve once his men had deserted him. Raymond brought up his Luger slowly, taking careful aim. He fired once.

The heavy Luger shell smashed into Kirk's vitals, splintering his ribs, boring into his heart. He staggered back, his gun dropping from nerveless fingers. His face went white and blood frothed at his mouth. He dropped in the street, groaning as he died.

Raymond swivelled round to cover the other cops. Seeing their chief killed, they lost heart, turned and ran. Raymond let them go. His lip curled; they were small fry, unimportant. But he had to get Traill before the gambler set up another stooge to run the police force.

His Cadillac was out of action. Raymond borrowed the police wagon. He headed south down Main Street, passing Elsa's house and Grant Street. He drove through the slum area, out into open country. He travelled fast, heading for Fawkes' house by the river that was where he expected to find Nick Traill. The west wind rose in force, sighing through the trees, blowing up for a gale.

Raymond reached the house. As he went towards the front door, he heard a shot. He changed direction, made for a French window. He started to run. A woman's scream shrilled out, long-drawn and intense with agony.

Raymond moved faster, sweating. That scream did something to his stomach.

Elsa was paying for her double-cross. He reached the French window and sprang into the room.

★   ★   ★

Elsa reclined on a divan in a downstairs room of Dr. Fawkes' cream and chromium house. Her blonde hair curled about her shoulders and her face was newly painted and powdered. She was smoking a cigarette through a long holder and laughing softly.

'I guess Nick's nice and cold by this time — Raymond was kinda fond of the Peters' dame. He wouldn't let anything stop him getting Nick.'

Fawkes' voice boomed jovially.

'So that leaves you free for me, Elsa.'

'I guess you know I've always been jealous of Nick.'

She let him kiss her, then replaced the cigarette holder between her lips. Fawkes' hearty manner didn't bluff her one bit. So he was bald on top and wore tweeds — so what? He made plenty of money out of his blackmail and seance rackets. And money was one thing that Elsa respected. She thought she'd team up with Fawkes.

'You going to be nice to me?' Fawkes asked.

She crushed out her cigarette and smiled.

'I'll think about it.'

'Elsa, dear — '

He broke off, turned abruptly at the sound of footfalls. The French window burst open and two men came into the room. Nick Traill's swarthy face was livid with rage; he showed his teeth. Verd's cold blue eyes glittered with lust to kill.

Fawkes came to his feet, blood draining from his face.

He stammered: 'Hello Nick. Glad to see you.'

Traill jeered: 'Yeah? Sure I'm not stopping you having fun?

The blonde came off the divan with fear in her eyes.

'Nick! I thought — '

Traill hit her across the mouth, knocking her across the room.

'You thought I was dead, you double-crossing bitch. Well, I'm not — and I'm here to settle the score.'

Fawkes said: 'Nick, I wasn't crossing you with your dame. I wouldn't do that. Only I thought you were interested in the Peters' girl.'

'Shut up!' Traill rapped. 'O'Connor shot up my gang. I'd have bought it if Kirk hadn't turned up. You and Elsa put him on to me.'

Elsa said, her face white: 'Not me, Nick. I wouldn't do a thing like that. It must have been Raymond — that rat has been poking his nose in again. He's the cause of all the trouble in Lynx Falls.'

Traill hit her again, leaving a red weal across her cheek.

'Yeah — and who told Raymond where to find me? You were the only one who knew I was hiding out at Underhill's place — I've figured that much. And now I'm going to even things up. You know what happens to doublecrossers, Elsa.'

The blonde shivered at the venom in Traill's voice. Verd said:

'Shall I let them have it?'

Nick Traill shook his head. He laughed, fingering his scar.

'There's no hurry,' he said, 'now that we're all together again. I want them to suffer first. Killing's too easy for rats like these.'

'Not me, Nick,' Fawkes pleaded. 'I swear I don't know anything about a doublecross. It must have been Elsa — '

'You lousy heel,' the blonde shrieked. 'It was you who put the idea in my head.'

Verd laughed unpleasantly.

'They sure give each other away,' he said. 'What you gonna do with 'em, boss?'

Traill's hand came out from his coat pocket, holding a long knife with a glittering blade. He ran his finger along the edge, smiling viciously.

'See the scar on my cheek? A knife did that. Now I'm going to use a knife — on Elsa's face!'

She went back to the wall, shaking with fear. There was something about Traill's eyes — a hint of madness — which alarmed her. He glided towards her, moving the knife in a gleaming arc, hissing:

'You first, Elsa. I'm gonna carve your face so no man will want to look at you again. But that won't worry you — because you aren't going to live long afterwards. Then I'll settle with the good doctor.'

Verd laughed. He leaned against the wall, lit a cigarette, waiting for the fun to start. Fawkes was desperate. Nick scared him, but he didn't have a gun handy. Verd was between him and the door. His eyes revolved round the room; Traill had his back to him, concentrating on the blonde.

Dr. Fawkes lunged forward. He hit Traill across the back of the neck. The gambler stumbled; and Fawkes got the knife. He turned on Verd.

The cleft-chinned gunman dodged the blade. He turned aside, dropping his cigarette and cursing; he went for his gun. Fawkes stabbed again; the blade caught Verd in the shoulder as he moved aside. His gun came up in a lightning movement and he thrust the barrel into Fawkes' mouth, choking him.

Fawkes tried to get away, but he was too late. Verd jerked the trigger twice. The shots sounded muffled. Two slugs crashed into his skull; his scream was choked. He slumped to the floor, blood pouring from his mouth. He died instantly.

Elsa made a rush for the door. Verd hit her across the side of the head, knocking her to the floor. She lay there, half-stunned; realized her desperate position and tried to crawl away.

Nick Traill had recovered from Fawkes' attack. He swore horribly and went for his knife. Verd was covering Elsa with his gun, trying to ease the pain in his shoulder. Traill got his knife and hurled himself at the blonde, pinning her to the floor.

He held the blade to her face, grated:

'This is it, Elsa. You won't doublecross anyone again.'

She screamed, tried to break free. But Nick was too strong; he forced her arms back over her head, gripped her wrists. She writhed, twisting and turning on the floor.

Traill brought down the tip of the knife blade and pricked her cheek. He leaned on the haft. The cold steel sank into her face. Elsa shrieked under the burning agony. Nick pulled out the knife to stab again.

Elsa bit his wrist, jerked sideways. Blood ran down her face into her mouth. It tasted of salt. Traill, cursing, lunged forward. Elsa, struggling to get away, caught the steel in her heart. Her screams stopped abruptly. She heaved once, shuddered, and went limp. She lay still, not breathing any more.

Traill left the knife haft protruding from her chest like a grotesque ornament. He stood up, panting.

Verd said: 'She won't rat on you again, boss.'

Traill said: 'Let's get out of here.'

They moved towards the door as Bill Raymond came through the French window, gun in hand. He saw Fawkes, his head half-blown away, and Elsa, white and still, with the knife still sticking out of her.

His Luger came up, blasting a heavy slug at Traill. The gambler moved fast, throwing himself out of line. Verd's gun spoke. The bullet caught Raymond in the side, slewing him round. Verd's second shot missed him by inches. He rolled sideways, snapped a shot at the cleft-chinned gunman. He hit him in the shoulder, just high of the wound Fawkes had left with the knife.

Verd howled with pain; he emptied his

gun at Raymond, but his arm was wild. Raymond aimed carefully. He squeezed the trigger. Crimson flame stabbed from the Luger's muzzle; the crash echoed and re-echoed; acrid cordite fumes hazed the air.

The slug sped straight for Verd's heart. He went over backwards, arms outstretched, mouth open. He sprawled in a heap, blood staining his coat. The hard glitter went out of his blue eyes.

Nick Traill had drawn a gun; he blasted a shot at Raymond, but he was too jumpy to shoot accurately. Raymond turned away, fired back. His shot came too close for the gambler's nerve; Traill turned and ran.

He darted out through the French window, into the open, running for his car. Raymond's leg dragged; his side hurt where Verd's bullet had hit him. Gritting his teeth, he went after the gambler.

He reached the door, leaned against the frame. Traill was twenty yards away, almost at his car. Raymond brought up the Luger, aimed. He pumped lead towards Traill, but the wind was too strong. It carried his slugs to one side.

Traill panicked. He cast one glance behind, saw Raymond following relentlessly after him — and ran on. He passed the car and kept going. Raymond hurried as fast as his injured side would allow; he reloaded his gun as he went.

His leg throbbed with pain, but he kept on. He was thinking of Dot and how Nick Traill had forced her into marriage; he wanted to kill him. And nothing was going to stop him.

The west wind howled about his ears as he took up the chase. Traill had increased his lead, but he was out of condition. Already his lungs were gasping for air. He was forced to slow down. He turned, saw that Raymond was closing the gap between them, and started running again.

Raymond called: 'You yellow rat! Stay and shoot it out.'

Traill didn't answer. Raymond's fury frightened him; he couldn't face the detective. He ran on, towards the river. Raymond plodded after him, face grim, determined to settle with the last of the Lynx Falls gangsters.

13

The west wind drove black, menacing clouds across the sky. Large drops of rain began to fall. Raymond hurried across the sand dunes towards the river Lynx; behind him, the hills were dark and obscure. He caught a glimpse of Nick Traill, still running.

Although it was only late afternoon, the sky was already dark. The wind howled ominously and heavy, brooding clouds blotted out the sun. A storm was blowing up. The rain came in gusts, borne on the wings of the gale.

Raymond kept moving; his side was a dull ache and rain lashed his face with a bitter fury. Only his burning desire for revenge drove him on. The Luger was heavy in his hand; it wanted to spray lead into the swarthy, scarred face of the gambler.

Traill reached the river. He stumbled over the sand, following the curve of the river towards the lake. Ahead of him, the falls made a roaring shower of foam and spray, magnificent and terrifying. He kept turning round to see the grim figure of Raymond, relentlessly plodding after him. Twice, Nick Traill stopped to shoot at his Nemesis; both times, the raging wind tore his bullets wide of the mark.

It was black as midnight; sombre clouds smothered everything in a blanket of gloom. The storm broke in a sultry barrage of thunder; it rolled like a thousand booming drums and lightning forked and flickered across the heavens. The rain became a tropical deluge; water swamped the air, making it difficult to breathe.

Raymond's clothes were soaked, sticking to his skin. He could barely see his way forward. Lightning stabbed the darkness, giving him a brief glimpse of Traill as the gambler staggered on. The noise of the falls was like a whirling, rushing maelstrom, blotting out everything except the thunder.

Traill was making for the bridge above the falls, the bridge that crossed the river.

If he could reach it ahead of Raymond, he was safe. The bridge was a slender network of steel, shivering in the wind. It was narrow and one man, armed, could hold it as long as his ammunition held out. Traill planned to wait for the detective and shoot him down as he attempted to cross the bridge.

A torrent of rain turned the sand to mud. Raymond's feet bogged down to the ankles. He slithered over the slippery surface, cursing and dashing water from his eyes. Traill still held his lead; he was nearly at the bridge now.

Raymond skidded on a muddy patch; his injured leg gave out and he sprawled on the ground, soaking in icy water. The Luger shot from his hand and disappeared in the darkness. He couldn't stop to hunt for it; he staggered upright, wincing with fresh pain in his side, and went on, unarmed.

Nick Traill came to the bridge over the river. He stopped, watched it swaying dangerously in the gale; he shuddered, but there was no turning back now. With Raymond right behind him, he needed every piece of advantage he could get.

He stepped on to the bridge, clinging to the handrail. Slowly, he moved forward, out across the river. The noise of the falls was deafening. Spray hit him like a million tiny needles pricking his skin. He reached the centre of the slender steel bridge, crouched low, waiting. He bared his teeth as he saw Raymond start to follow him over the swinging net of steel. He brought up his gun, held it level. He waited for Raymond to move nearer.

Bill Raymond started across the bridge. He was cold and wet. The gale howled and rain and spray from the falls showered over him. Peals of thunder sounded like an echo of the roaring torrent that passed over the falls, to drop into the lower stretch of river, fifty feet below. Lightning flickered and he saw the gambler waiting for him.

Traill was twenty feet away, a menacing figure crouched on the steel platform in space. The gun in his hand glistened wetly. Raymond gritted his teeth and went on. It was dark again. He dropped to his knees and crawled forward on all fours. Unless the lightning came again, Traill wouldn't see him until he was right on top of him.

Raymond shortened the gap between them. Even through the noise of the falls and the thunder, he could hear the steel plates of the bridge creaking and groaning under the strain. The bridge swayed dangerously. An overhead cable snapped and the hawser curled like a snake, lashing the air. If the bridge collapsed, they would both plunge to death.

He crawled through the blackness, praying that the lightning would not come again. He still could not see Traill, but he knew he was there, somewhere ahead, gun in hand, waiting with murder in his heart.

Thunder rolled — and lightning flashed. Raymond hurled himself forward. He saw Traill's swarthy face dripping with water, the long scar livid on his cheek. Traill's gun arm swung up; his finger tightened round the trigger. The hammer clicked uselessly; in the downpour of rain, the cartridge chamber had been soaked, rendering the gun useless.

Raymond grappled desperately. Traill used the gun as a club, beating at Raymond's head and screaming wildly. The gun hit Raymond's injured side, paralysing him with agonizing pain. He fell back, helpless. Traill got on top of him and smashed the gun in his face.

Raymond spat out blood and rolled against the steel handrail. He felt the bridge quiver as the gale tore at its flimsy structure. Traill struck again; Raymond fended off the blow with his arm. He got a grip on the gambler's gun-hand, forced the gun from his grasp. The wind carried it into the froth of foam below.

Traill had his hands round Raymond's throat; he squeezed with all his strength, snarling like a wild-cat. Raymond gasped for air; his strength began to leave him. Urgently, he smashed his fist hard against Traill's aquiline nose, brought up his knee into the gambler's stomach. Traill moaned; and released his death-hold.

Raymond moved clear. In the darkness, he lost touch with Traill. He crawled forward — and got a boot in his face. Traill wanted to get away. He was scared of the bridge collapsing; even more frightened of the desperate man who wouldn't give up. Raymond came at him for the kill. His eyes burned with hatred as he thought of Dot and the way Nick Traill had treated her. Revenge flamed through him, possessed him. He was going to kill . . .

He got his arms round Traill's body in a bear-hug. They rocked to and fro on the swinging bridge, the gale howling about them, rain streaming down their faces. Trail weakened; he sagged. Raymond's injured leg gave out and they both fell, rolling over and over, exchanging punches. The bridge creaked ominously.

Traill began to scream with terror.

'The bridge — it's breaking up! Let go, you fool . . . we'll both be killed!'

He tore himself free in a frenzy of desperation, started to run for safety. Raymond caught his ankle, tripped him. A steel cable snapped . . . and another. Raymond ignored his danger — Traill *had* to die. He grappled with him again.

Traill smashed his fists in Raymond's face, screaming: 'Let go — let go! The bridge is falling — '

Raymond clung on. He felt the bridge sag beneath him. The gale tore at the hand-rail, ripped it away. Another strut collapsed. The bridge tilted at an angle and they slid towards the edge. One final fury of the gale destroyed the bridge's last support. It buckled like a matchbox under a power-press, crumpled in a tangle of steel lattice-work — and dropped into the water fifty feet below.

Raymond, still maintaining his grip on Nick Traill, was flung clear of the wreckage. Lightning flashed and forked across the sky. He saw the boiling fury of the falls rush up to meet them, twisted the gambler's body under him. A froth of foam submerged them. Rocks, jagged and diamond-hard, loomed up through the water.

Traill's body hit a rock. Something inside him snapped. Raymond missed most of the shock. He hung on grimly as the water swept him down-river. He bobbed helplessly in the raging stream, gasping for breath. He began to black-out. A dark mist enveloped him and all the strength went out of his body . . . he was unconscious when the river tossed him on a sand bank.

★ ★ ★

Raymond opened his eyes to a clear, moonlit sky. The gale had blown itself out and the rain had stopped. He felt limp and weak and he couldn't think straight. He tried to get up but his hands were fixed rigidly about something. He looked down.

He was still gripping Nick Traill's body. The gambler's back and neck were broken and he was cold and stiff in death. Raymond forced himself to let go. He staggered upright, testing his limbs. The gun-wound in his side gave him pain when he moved.

The river, swollen to flood-tide, swirled a little way away. He started to walk across the sand dunes to the road. With Traill dead, his job in Lynx Falls was ended; the last of the gangsters had paid in full for his life of crime. Living violently, he had died the same way.

Raymond began to think of Dot Peters, and his heart glowed with a warmth he had never known before.

He limped along the road. Someone would come with a car, then he would get a lift back to town, to Northwood and Dot. He shivered a little with cold, felt in his pocket automatically for cigarettes; threw away the sodden package.

He watched the road. The headlamps of a car gleamed through the dusk. He signalled it with his arm and the car stopped.

★   ★   ★

A month later, Bill Raymond drove through Lynx Falls. The town had a different atmosphere. Afternoon sunlight gleamed on newly cleaned sidewalks, the shop windows were polished, and even the trees in Central Plaza tried to put out a few green shoots.

Elsa's girls, the last remaining crooks of Traill's mob, had beat it out of town. City Hall wore a new facade of white stone and the Chief of Police was a grizzled veteran with a sense of law and order. Peace had come to Lynx Falls.

Waiting for the traffic lights to change, Raymond's eyes smiled as he saw a cop on duty. The cop was smartly dressed; he wore a cap and his buttons glistened brightly in the sun.

Raymond drove up Main Street. The new *Gazette* office was almost complete; the Palace hotel showed both white stone and gilt. Even the drab apartment blocks seemed a little brighter.

He reached Northwood and wrought iron gates with the name: 'PETERS.' He swung his car into the drive, up to the brown stone house. Flowers made a gay pattern on the lawn.

The scrubbed stone lions on each side of the door welcomed him. He hung on the bell rope and listened to distant chimes. The servant smiled:

'Good afternoon, Mister Raymond. A lovely day, if I may say so. You'll find Miss Peters and Mr. Goodrich in the library.'

Raymond went across the pale blue and cream tiled hall, threw his hat at a wall peg with carefree ease; he ringed it first time. He surveyed himself in the mirror; his bronzed face was freshly shaven; his new suit fitted well and the rose in his button-hole was just the right shade of red. Whistling happily, he went through the oak panelled door, into the library.

Dot Peters said: 'Bill, darling!'

A white silk dress made a lovely contrast with her dark, wavy hair. Her eyes smiled under long lashes and her face lit up with an inner rapture. She slipped into Raymond's arms and tilted her full, carmined lips for him to kiss. Raymond obliged her and enjoyed doing it.

Jerry Goodrich yawned in a bored way. He said:

'When you two love-birds have finished billing and cooing, maybe we can get down to business. You may have forgotten I have a paper to edit.'

Raymond and Dot sat side by side on the settee. Raymond kept his arm about the girl's waist, holding her close.

Goodrich regarded them from behind the curve of his pipe. His eyes twinkled behind thick-lensed spectacles.

'Love,' he said drily, 'it's wonderful! If only I'd thought to give her lilies.'

Raymond grinned.

'I've told you before, if you had blood, instead of printer's ink in your veins — '

Dot scolded: 'Stop it! I won't have you quarrelling on my wedding eve.'

Jerry Goodrich tossed a paper at Raymond. 'A preview of tomorrow's write-up,' he said.

Raymond took the paper and read:

A NOTABLE WEDDING

At Lynx Falls Parish Church, this afternoon, Mr. William Raymond, of New York, will marry Miss Dorothy Peters, only daughter of the late Nathaniel Peters. Mr. Raymond is well-known and liked as the private detective who did so much to rid our town of its gangsters and crooked administration.

It is, perhaps, not so well known that Miss Peters has relinquished all claims to her father's fortune, insisting that the money be used for the betterment of the town. We know *that all our readers will join us in wishing the happy pair all the luck in the world. Mr. Jeremy Goodrich, editor of the Gazette, will perform the offices of best man . . .*

There was a lot more, detailing his handling of the gangs, and how he had brought death to the leaders, one by one. Raymond handed back the paper, laughing.

'You make me feel like one of the old Greek heroes!'

Dot said: 'You are, to me. If it hadn't been for you, I'd never be able to look the people of Lynx Falls in the face. I believe they've even forgiven my father.'

Raymond watched her face. He was delighted to find that the freckle on the side of her snub nose fascinated him as much as it had when he'd first discovered it. He leaned towards her and kissed the freckle.

'Disgusting!' Jerry said with mock horror.

Raymond said: 'You're jealous because I'm marrying the loveliest girl in Lynx Falls.'

Dot blushed happily. She pressed Raymond's hand, and said:

'Bill, my annulment papers came through this morning. My forced marriage to Nick Traill has been crossed off the record.'

Raymond nodded.

'I hope you won't want to get out of this one.'

'Silly!'

Dot snuggled closer.

'You just *try* to get away!' she said severely. Jerry laughed.

'You've had it, Bill. She won't let go now — you're hooked. For life,' he added.

The editor drew on his pipe.

'You've done a good job in Lynx Falls, Bill. The town badly needed cleaning up. Now, we're rid of the lot of them; Traill, Archer, O'Connor, Fawkes — you've made a clean sweep, and we can start over again to build a decent, respectable town.'

Dot shuddered.

'Don't let's talk about the past — we've the future to think of. Tomorrow!'

She turned to Raymond, asked anxiously:

with black velvet and heavy curtains blocked out the sunlight. Spluttering candles gave a faint yellow light and an exotic perfume.

Fawkes was sprawled in a chair at the hub from which the semi-circle of chairs radiated. His eyes were closed and his voice came out in a high-pitched squeak. Raymond guessed he had gate-crashed one of the blackmailer's seances.

The squeaky voice complained:

'I feel a disturbing influence in the room . . . '

Raymond grated: 'Like hell you do! I'm looking for Nick Traill. Elsa will do — '

Fawkes' body shuddered; he writhed as if in a trance. A woman grabbed Raymond's arm and dragged him to an empty chair.

She shushed angrily: 'Be quiet, young man! It's dangerous to distract a medium when he's in trance. Your mundane business will have to wait.'

The others in the group glared at Raymond. Fawkes' voice came again, high-pitched and squeaky as he simulated his spirit-guide:

'I have a message for someone in the room. A man.'

Raymond tensed. Something told him that Fawkes was taking this method of telling him what he wanted to know. He loathed the idea of sitting still and pandering to Fawkes' trickery, but he had to hear what the man said.

The voice went on: 'The message comes from a girl with fair hair . . . ' Elsa, Raymond guessed. ' . . . she wants him to know that the person he seeks has taken refuge with a man of law. Her thoughts are most violent — I feel I cannot go on . . . '

Raymond came out of his seat, ignoring the woman who tried to hold him down. Underhill! Fawkes had told him that Nick Traill was at the lawyer's house. Elsa must have had a row with Nick — obviously over Dot. The blonde wanted him to kill Nick; that was the reference to 'violent thoughts.'

He smiled; Elsa was going to get her wish. Raymond went through the door to the passage. In the hall, he found a telephone. He used it.

'Your leg's all right now, Bill?'

Goodrich threw up his hands in disgust.

'Bill only got a flesh wound,' he complained. 'Me — I'm just out of hospital, but nobody asks me how I am. Nobody cares about *me*.'

Raymond said: 'You're not the bridegroom!'

He took Dot in his arms and kissed her long and hard. They were so wrapped up in each other they didn't hear Goodrich rise to leave.

'It is obvious,' he said to himself, because no-one else was listening, 'that my presence is no longer required.'

He went out, closing the door behind him. Dot sighed happily, secure in Raymond's arms. They weren't disturbed for a long time.

Outside, the west wind dropped to a gentle breeze. It might blow again — but never again would the west wind bring terror to Lynx Falls. Peace had come to the town.

We do hope that you have enjoyed reading this large print book.

Did you know that all of our titles are available for purchase?

We publish a wide range of high quality large print books including:
Romances, Mysteries, Classics
General Fiction
Non Fiction and Westerns

Special interest titles available in large print are:
The Little Oxford Dictionary
Music Book, Song Book
Hymn Book, Service Book

Also available from us courtesy of Oxford University Press:
Young Readers' Dictionary
(large print edition)
Young Readers' Thesaurus
(large print edition)

For further information or a free brochure, please contact us at:
Ulverscroft Large Print Books Ltd.,
The Green, Bradgate Road, Anstey,
Leicester, LE7 7FU, England.
Tel: (00 44) **0116 236 4325**
Fax: (00 44) **0116 234 0205**

'Love,' he said drily, 'it's wonderful! If only I'd thought to give her lilies.'

Raymond grinned.

'I've told you before, if you had blood, instead of printer's ink in your veins — '

Dot scolded: 'Stop it! I won't have you quarrelling on my wedding eve.'

Jerry Goodrich tossed a paper at Raymond.

'A preview of tomorrow's write-up,' he said.

Raymond took the paper and read:

A NOTABLE WEDDING

At Lynx Falls Parish Church, this afternoon, Mr. William Raymond, of New York, will marry Miss Dorothy Peters, only daughter of the late Nathaniel Peters. Mr. Raymond is well-known and liked as the private detective who did so much to rid our town of its gangsters and crooked administration.

It is, perhaps, not so well known that Miss Peters has relinquished all claims to her father's fortune, insisting that the money be used for the betterment of the town. We know time. He surveyed himself in the mirror; his bronzed face was freshly shaven; his new suit fitted well and the rose in his button-hole was just the right shade of red. Whistling happily, he went through the oak panelled door, into the library.

Dot Peters said: 'Bill, darling!'

A white silk dress made a lovely contrast with her dark, wavy hair. Her eyes smiled under long lashes and her face lit up with an inner rapture. She slipped into Raymond's arms and tilted her full, carmined lips for him to kiss. Raymond obliged her and enjoyed doing it.

Jerry Goodrich yawned in a bored way. He said:

'When you two love-birds have finished billing and cooing, maybe we can get down to business. You may have forgotten I have a paper to edit.'

Raymond and Dot sat side by side on the settee. Raymond kept his arm about the girl's waist, holding her close.

Goodrich regarded them from behind the curve of his pipe. His eyes twinkled behind thick-lensed spectacles.

of the bridge collapsing; even more frightened of the desperate man who wouldn't give up. Raymond came at him for the kill. His eyes burned with hatred as he thought of Dot and the way Nick Traill had treated her. Revenge flamed through him, possessed him. He was going to kill . . .

He got his arms round Traill's body in a bear-hug. They rocked to and fro on the swinging bridge, the gale howling about them, rain streaming down their faces. Trail weakened; he sagged. Raymond's injured leg gave out and they both fell, rolling over and over, exchanging punches. The bridge creaked ominously.

Traill began to scream with terror.

'The bridge — it's breaking up! Let go, you fool . . . we'll both be killed!'

He tore himself free in a frenzy of desperation, started to run for safety. Raymond caught his ankle, tripped him. A steel cable snapped . . . and another. Raymond ignored his danger — Traill *had* to die. He grappled with him again.

Traill smashed his fists in Raymond's face, screaming: 'Let go — let go! The

Raymond grappled desperately. Traill used the gun as a club, beating at Raymond's head and screaming wildly. The gun hit Raymond's injured side, paralysing him with agonizing pain. He fell back, helpless. Traill got on top of him and smashed the gun in his face.

Raymond spat out blood and rolled against the steel handrail. He felt the bridge quiver as the gale tore at its flimsy structure. Traill struck again; Raymond fended off the blow with his arm. He got a grip on the gambler's gun-hand, forced the gun from his grasp. The wind carried it into the froth of foam below.

Traill had his hands round Raymond's throat; he squeezed with all his strength, snarling like a wild-cat. Raymond gasped for air; his strength began to leave him. Urgently, he smashed his fist hard against Traill's aquiline nose, brought up his knee into the gambler's stomach. Traill moaned; and released his death-hold.

Raymond moved clear. In the darkness, he lost touch with Traill. He crawled forward — and got a boot in his face. Traill wanted to get away. He was scared fours. Unless the lightning came again, Traill wouldn't see him until he was right on top of him.

Raymond shortened the gap between them. Even through the noise of the falls and the thunder, he could hear the steel plates of the bridge creaking and groaning under the strain. The bridge swayed dangerously. An overhead cable snapped and the hawser curled like a snake, lashing the air. If the bridge collapsed, they would both plunge to death.

He crawled through the blackness, praying that the lightning would not come again. He still could not see Traill, but he knew he was there, somewhere ahead, gun in hand, waiting with murder in his heart.

Thunder rolled — and lightning flashed. Raymond hurled himself forward. He saw Traill's swarthy face dripping with water, the long scar livid on his cheek. Traill's gun arm swung up; his finger tightened round the trigger. The hammer clicked uselessly; in the downpour of rain, the cartridge chamber had been soaked, rendering the gun useless.

every piece of advantage he could get.

He stepped on to the bridge, clinging to the handrail. Slowly, he moved forward, out across the river. The noise of the falls was deafening. Spray hit him like a million tiny needles pricking his skin. He reached the centre of the slender steel bridge, crouched low, waiting. He bared his teeth as he saw Raymond start to follow him over the swinging net of steel. He brought up his gun, held it level. He waited for Raymond to move nearer.

Bill Raymond started across the bridge. He was cold and wet. The gale howled and rain and spray from the falls showered over him. Peals of thunder sounded like an echo of the roaring torrent that passed over the falls, to drop into the lower stretch of river, fifty feet below. Lightning flickered and he saw the gambler waiting for him.

Traill was twenty feet away, a menacing figure crouched on the steel platform in space. The gun in his hand glistened wetly. Raymond gritted his teeth and went on. It was dark again. He dropped to his knees and crawled forward on all

197